KIDZ BOP® PLUS ONE

A JUNIOR NOVEL

Join the **KIDZ BOP**®
*Kids as They Hit the
Road to Find Their
Newest Member*

Bethany Bryan

Aadamsmedia
Avon, Massachusetts

Published by
Adams Media, a division of F+W Media, Inc.
57 Littlefield Street, Avon, MA 02322. U.S.A.
www.adamsmedia.com

ISBN 10: 1-4405-0574-8
ISBN 13: 978-1-4405-0574-4
eISBN 10: 1-4405-0898-4
eISBN 13: 978-1-4405-0898-1

Printed by RR Donnelley, Harrisonburg, VA, US

10 9 8 7 6 5 4 3 2 1

June 2011

Library of Congress Cataloging-in-Publication Data
is available from the publisher.

This publication is designed to provide accurate and authoritative information
with regard to the subject matter covered. It is sold with the understanding that the
publisher is not engaged in rendering legal, accounting, or other professional advice.
If legal advice or other expert assistance is required, the services of a competent
professional person should be sought.

—From a *Declaration of Principles* jointly adopted by a Committee of the
American Bar Association and a Committee of Publishers and Associations

Many of the designations used by manufacturers and sellers to distinguish their
product are claimed as trademarks. Where those designations appear in this book
and Adams Media was aware of a trademark claim, the designations have been
printed with initial capital letters.

This book is available at quantity discounts for bulk purchases.
For information, please call 1-800-289-0963.

PART 1

Chapter 1
Goodbye Hometown, Hello KIDZ BOP!

Eva stood by the tall window of the hotel suite and looked out over Times Square. New York City may be her hometown, but she still got a thrill every time she saw the bright lights and flashing neon of the most exciting entertainment intersection in the world.

Eva lived only a short cab ride away—so she was the first of the KIDZ BOP Kids to arrive. As the only New Yorker, she volunteered to come early, and help Chloe decorate the suite for the other kids.

"Soon, you KIDZ BOP Kids will have your own marquee," said Chloe, joining Eva at the window. "Pretty cool, huh?"

Chloe was the KIDZ BOP manager, a tiny powerhouse of a woman who left a career as a choreographer on Broadway to take over the group—and turn them into a dancing, singing musical sensation.

"Amazing." Eva shook her long dark curls. "I can't wait to meet everybody and get started."

"We have a lot of work to do." Chloe smiled. "I see you came prepared."

Steffan, Hanna, Charisma, and Elijah were flying in from all over the country—and Eva wanted to welcome them in style. Her mom was a fashion designer, so she knew a thing or two about style. She'd raided their private party stock for crepe paper, posters, glitter, baubles, and balloons—and armed with all that, Eva planned to transform their suite into an awesome tour of the Big Apple as glitzy as the real-life spectacle outside their windows.

"Ready?" Eva switched on her iPod, and music blasted through the suite. "Let's get the party started!"

There was nothing Elijah liked better than a game of one-on-one with his dad. Sure, the odds were against him, as his father was a professional basketball player—not to mention nearly seven feet tall! But that didn't keep Elijah from enjoying himself or even from winning from time to time. What Elijah lacked in height and experience he made up for in energy and mischief.

They were out on the court behind their house, taking advantage of their last few minutes together.

"You're supposed to be packing for the trip." Dad tossed the basketball from one large hand to another, high above Elijah's head.

Elijah jumped, slapping his arm at the ball his father held just out of his reach. "Whatever I put in my backpack, Mom just refolds and repacks anyway. May as well play." He leapt again, a dancer's leap that brought him high enough to grab the ball.

Back on the ground, Elijah dribbled the basketball between his legs, feinted to the left of his dad, and then made a dash for the hoop. His dad scooped him up from behind, and lifted his son up to the rim, where he could slam the ball through the net.

"Let me go!" Elijah wriggled free, and swung from the hoop before dropping to the ground, landing in a squat.

"Are you all right?"

Elijah winced, but rose to his feet with a grin. "Fine. And ready for New York City!"

Hanna was glad that she was going to travel with Steffan. They were both from Denver, so their moms planned their flights to New York City together. Hanna had a twin brother, and two younger siblings, so she was used to being part of a pair. Life was more fun when you had a partner—whether you were traveling or singing or dancing or acting. That's why Hanna was so excited to be one of the KIDZ BOP Kids. With five of them performing together, they couldn't go wrong! But she worried about the group's uneven number—how would they pair up?

She recognized Steffan right away—he was the really cute guy with the guitar case. And he was talented, too—she'd seen his video on KIDZBOP.com singing great songs he'd written himself. He must be a good dancer, too, or he wouldn't be a KIDZ BOP Kid.

"Hi." Steffan smiled at her—pointed to the novel she held on her lap. "I see you're a Twilight fan. I'm a big reader, but I haven't read those yet. You'll have to tell me all about it."

"Oh, good. You can quiz me while we take off so I don't freak out." Hanna leaned in toward Steffan and whispered. "I've never flown before, and I'm a little nervous."

"Piece of cake," Steffan said with a bravado he didn't necessarily feel. Sure, flying on a plane was no big deal, but going to New York City to perform at Madison Square Garden was. Imagine, yesterday he was just another kid making videos on his webcam after school—and now he was a KIDZ BOP Kid getting ready to open for Madison Day! "Nothing to worry about."

Hanna grinned. It was going to be a great flight!

Charisma posed by the statue of film star John Wayne at the John Wayne airport in Orange County while her mother snapped yet another picture of her only daughter. Her mom seemed determined to document every second of Charisma's life. She loved her mom, but she was secretly glad that she'd be going to New York on her own—even if it was such a long flight to do solo.

"Okay, Mom, we have to go now." Charisma had never been to New York City; she'd never been east of the Rockies. She was a Western girl, who loved horses and country music and cheerleading. What would they think of her there? How would she fit in?

"You look worried, honey." Her mother walked over, camera in one hand, and smoothed Charisma's bangs with the other. "There's nothing to worry about. Just be yourself—and they'll love you."

"You always say that," Charisma said.

"That's because it's true." Her mom gave her a big hug. "Now go show New York City how we do it out West."

Steffan watched through the plane window as the Rocky Mountains disappeared in the distance. This was the saddest part of flying for him, looking out at his favorite mountains and knowing he was leaving them behind. This would be the first summer that he wouldn't spend most of his time hiking in the mountains with his friends or rafting on the Colorado River. He would be rehearsing and performing onstage with the other KIDZ BOP Kids. What outdoor activities would they have in New York City? Running from taxis?

It was Steffan's mom who had convinced him to audition.

"If I joined the KIDZ BOP Kids, I would have to leave Colorado and all my friends!" Steffan said, carefully tuning his guitar.

"Are you telling me you would pass up auditioning for something this amazing because you're afraid of getting in?" said Steffan's mom, looking at him over the rim of her glasses. It was the look she gave him when she thought he was talking crazy.

"Mike and I were talking about starting a band over the summer!" said Steffan.

"You can still start a band if you don't make the KIDZ BOP Kids," his mom replied.

That night, Steffan camped out in the backyard like he sometimes did when he needed to think about things. He had been waiting for an opportunity like this to come along for a long time. And now, here it was in front of him, and the whole thing was making him nuts. It was just an audition. If he didn't get in, he didn't get in. But he had to try, right? When Steffan woke up the next morning, he sat with his guitar in his lap as he gazed out at the mountain view from the family's backyard. The mountains would always be there. But getting to be a KIDZ BOP Kid was an opportunity that came once in a lifetime. Steffan knew what he had to do.

"Goodbye, Colorado! Hello, New York City!" said Hanna, snapping Steffan out of his daze. She grinned, but Steffan could still see her gripping the arms of her seat tightly.

"Hey," said Steffan, digging his camera out of his bag. "Pose for a photo with me, and we can send it back to our moms when we get to New York."

"Okay," said Hanna, doing her best to put on a brave face. "Anything to take my mind off being thousands of feet from the ground."

Chapter 2
New Faces, New Friends

Charisma didn't know if she should knock on the hotel room door that said, "Welcome KIDZ BOP Kids!" or if she should just go in using the room key they had given her at the desk downstairs. It felt strange to just walk in without knocking!

Charisma had felt very important as she walked down the ramp to baggage claim at the airport and saw a man holding a sign with her name on it. A driver, just for her? And it felt like something out of the movies as they drove into Manhattan in a long, black car and parked in front of the fanciest hotel Charisma had ever seen. But it wasn't until Charisma arrived at the door of the KIDZ BOP Kids suite that it really sank in. She was about to be a celebrity! And in a few weeks, they would be the opening act for *Madison Day* at Madison Square Garden.

Charisma checked for dust on her cowboy boots and smoothed her long, light brown hair away from her eyes.

But before Charisma could put her key in the slot, the door opened. The girl standing in the doorway was tall and had long, dark curly hair. Just like in the picture she had sent to Charisma when they began exchanging e-mails a month before.

"You're here!" said Eva. *"You're actually here!"*

Charisma practically threw herself at Eva, wrapping her in the biggest hug ever. The girls spun around in their excitement.

"You're early!" Eva said when they had calmed down. "I wanted the room to be all ready when you got here!"

"Welcome to New York, Charisma!" Chloe called from where she stood on a stepladder at the far end of the room, still holding the huge, glittery "Welcome!" banner she and Eva had been trying to tape to the wall. "Now . . . could someone give me a hand with this?"

"Broadway!" was the only word that had come out of Hanna's mouth since she and Steffan had stepped from their limo in Times Square. She looked around in awe. This was the moment she had been waiting for. *Mamma Mia! The Lion King! Wicked!* Hanna had memorized all their soundtracks and had dreamed of seeing them live. And now she was right in the heart of the theater district!

Hanna and Steffan both reached for their suitcases. The limo driver smiled and shooed them away. "Don't worry about these. We'll take care of them."

Steffan grabbed his guitar. "I'll take this one though," he said.

"No problem, sir," said the driver.

Steffan gave Hanna a sideways glance and grinned. "Sir?"

Hanna grabbed her backpack from the pile and she and Steffan headed through the revolving doors of the hotel.

One elevator ride later, they stood in front of the door of the KIDZ BOP suite. Somewhere inside, loud music was playing.

Elijah had wanted to fly by himself. No one else would be arriving with their parents. But Elijah's mom had insisted.

"What kind of mother would I be if I put you on a plane to a strange city by yourself?" she asked, unfolding the socks Elijah had packed into his duffel bag and carefully refolding them.

And now, rather than getting to enjoy a nice, pleasant flight with his headphones on, Elijah had to sit through listening to his mom remind him about the dangers of New York City.

Elijah was totally relieved when they finally landed in New York. His mom would be heading down to Brooklyn that night to hang out with Elijah's aunt and uncle for the weekend and then flying back to Detroit on Monday. Elijah had his fingers crossed that he would be too busy with rehearsal to spend any extra time with her. He imagined his mom trailing behind him to rehearsals and asking him to stop and pose for pictures every five seconds.

"Is someone knocking?" Charisma called to Eva.

"I didn't hear anything!" Eva replied.

The girls had spent the last half hour blasting the Ting Tings and blowing up party balloons, while Chloe finished stringing up some lights. And, at last, the KIDZ BOP suite looked worthy of the five kid celebs who would soon be residing there.

The walls were covered with posters of some of the great New York City landmarks. The Empire State Building, the Statue of Liberty, and Central Park lined the walls, surrounded by red and blue balloons and so many streamers it looked like one of the many New York City parades.

The New York look was completed by the sparkling red disco ball that Eva had hung from the ceiling. When the light hit it just right, the room lit up like a walk through Times Square at night.

"Well, what do you think?" said Eva, hitting pause on her iPod and gazing around the room. Chloe nodded with approval.

"It looks amazing," said Charisma, grinning at her friend.

"This," said Eva, "is New York City."

"It's *beautiful*!" said a voice.

Everyone turned to look at the dark-haired girl standing in the doorway.

"Hi," she said with an awkward wave, "I'm Hanna."

"*Hanna!*" Charisma and Eva screamed in unison.

"Don't forget about Steffan," Hanna said.

Steffan had been standing quietly in the doorway, watching the excitement unfold.

"Steffan!" said Charisma and hugged him as well.

"Well, we're almost complete," said Chloe. "I wonder where Elijah could be."

Elijah was in a limo two blocks away listening to his mom talk about the best ways to avoid pick-pocketers.

"And whatever you do," Elijah's mom said, "never carry your wallet in your back pocket."

"Back pockets bad. Front pockets good. Got it," Elijah said.

"Well, then. The last thing I'm going to say is have fun," said Elijah's mom. "And call us if you need anything."

"I will," Elijah said, stifling a yawn.

"Well, guess what. We have arrived," said Elijah's mom, gazing out the window of the limo and up at the towering hotel.

Elijah could barely remember the lobby or elevator he took to the KIDZ BOP suite. He only became aware of his surroundings again when he knocked on the door. When it opened, Elijah came face to face with the other four KIDZ BOP Kids for the first time.

Chapter 3
On the Loose in the Big Apple

"**G**et up, sleepyheads!" Eva said, popping her head into Steffan and Elijah's room in the KIDZ BOP suite.

Elijah pulled his pillow back over his face. "We aren't starting rehearsal until tomorrow!" he groaned.

"We're not rehearsing today," Eva replied. "I have something better planned."

Steffan, who was sharing the room with Elijah moaned, "I'm still on Mountain Time, and it's only 6 A.M. in Denver," before rolling over and closing his eyes again.

"And I'm on Detroit time . . . and there it's still time to sleep," said Elijah.

"Okay, then I guess you're going to miss out on the waffles Chloe made . . . and my surprise," said Eva, and left the room.

"How'd it go?" said Chloe when Eva returned to the tiny kitchen where Chloe was making breakfast.

"Give them about five minutes. No one can resist the word 'surprise.'" Four minutes later, Elijah and Steffan were in the kitchen eating waffles at the table.

"Well? What's the surprise?" asked Charisma.

Eva grinned and clapped her hands with glee. "I'm taking you all on a sightseeing tour of New York!"

"Ooooooh!" said Hanna, "Can we go to the MoMA?" The MoMA was the Museum of Modern Art. Hanna's mom was an art teacher, so Hanna had spent most of her childhood with art books open in her lap, studying every painting she saw.

"Yes!" said Eva. "In fact, I printed out lists for all of you with things we can do in New York. Everybody gets to pick one, and we'll go see it today."

Elijah picked up the list. Okay, this was going to be cool. Now, he could visit the Apollo Theater. He'd been watching the stand-up specials since he could push the buttons on a remote control. And now he had a chance to see it in person!

Steffan looked at the list with a faraway look in his eyes. He was going to get to see Strawberry Fields, the memorial to his idol, John Lennon.

"Well, I want to see the Empire State Building!" said Charisma cheerfully. "I want to see the whole city at once. What floor is it?"

"The eighty-sixth floor," said Eva. "And we can absolutely go."

"What about you, Eva?" said Elijah with a grin. "Do you get to pick a place as well?"

Eva smiled. "Of course. We're going to my favorite place in the whole city."

"What about you, Chloe?" asked Elijah.

"We're already in my favorite part of the city," said Chloe, picking up a plate from the table. "Broadway. The theater district."

"Well, what are we waiting for? I'm ready to see New York!" said Elijah.

The five KIDZ BOP Kids were lined up on the observation deck of the Empire State Building looking out at the city.

"I can see the Statue of Liberty from up here! She's about this big!" said Hanna, indicating with her fingers.

"Look at the people down there. They're like ants," said Elijah. "You know what I could use right now?"

"What's that?" said Steffan.

"A water balloon," said Elijah, slyly.

"Don't even think about it!" said Chloe, raising one eyebrow.

"Well, what do you think, Charisma?" asked Eva.

"It's *unbelievable*!" said Charisma with a sigh.

"All of you get together and I'll take your picture," said Chloe. The KIDZ BOP Kids gathered into a line.

"Say 'we love New York!'" said Chloe and snapped the photo.

"Aw, our first official photo as KIDZ BOP Kids," said Hanna. She loved a good photo op.

"Well," said Eva, "Are we ready for the Apollo Theater?"

"*Woo!*" said Elijah, raising his fists in the air in excitement.

The KIDZ BOP Kids hopped the subway and headed to Harlem, home of the world-famous Apollo Theater.

"Do you know how many famous people got their start at the Apollo?" asked Elijah. He had talked about the Apollo from the moment they stepped on the elevator that took them back down to the first floor of the Empire State Building and on the walk to the subway. As the KIDZ BOP Kids and Chloe settled into their seats on the subway, Elijah's excitement only seemed to increase. But as they climbed the steps of the A train and got to the street, Elijah seemed to be shaking with excitement.

"There it is!" Elijah said when the theater came into sight. "Someone get my picture standing in front of it! Everyone back home is going to be so jealous!"

"All right, but we'd better hurry inside. I have a big surprise for you," said Chloe.

"I only hurry for huge surprises," said Elijah, posing for a photo. "Is it huge?"

Chloe rolled her eyes.

The surprise was being allowed to stand center stage at the Apollo Theater. Elijah could not believe his luck.

"How did you get them to let me do this?" asked Elijah.

"Let's just say I know people and leave it at that," Chloe replied with a smile.

"Look at me! I'm Chris Rock!" said Elijah and broke into his stand-up routine.

"I think we're supposed to heckle him now," said Charisma. "Boo! Hiss!"

"Who's this guy?" said Steffan. "Bring on the comedian!"

"Yeah, yeah," said Elijah, waving them off. "Everybody's a critic."

"Well, are you ready to see the MoMA?" Eva asked, leaning over to ask Hanna quietly.

"*Yes*," said Hanna.

"Good," said Eva, "because we're going there next."

Meeting the other KIDZ BOP Kids was an amazing experience. But nothing compared, for Hanna, to wandering around the MoMA and seeing the work of all of her favorite artists . . . *in person*.

"Andy Warhol," said Hanna, dreamily, admiring one of her favorite paintings that was hanging in the gallery.

"You should get a print of this for your bedroom back home," said Eva, admiring the painting. "I think they have some in the gift shop."

"Ohh, awesome idea!" said Hanna. She had immediately liked Eva when meeting her in person. When she found out that they would be sharing a bedroom, she was thrilled. Eva had a huge collection of hats and shoes, and she loved to share. The night before, they had stayed up late talking about their new life as KIDZ BOP Kids.

"So," Hanna continued, "what's your favorite New York site and when do we get to go there?"

Eva laughed. "Bloomingdale's, of course. And right after this."

Charisma loved shopping, but she had never been to a store quite like Bloomingdale's. For one thing, it was enormous. But more importantly, Charisma was surrounded by an unlimited number of things she would love to own. Lip gloss! A new pair of leather boots! Sunglasses! Hats!

"I want *everything*," Charisma announced.

"Well, why don't you just settle for this scarf?" said Eva from behind her. "This shade of green would look great on you."

Steffan, on the other hand, was not into shopping at all. He felt like a fish out of water in the fancy department store. He purchased most of his clothes from his favorite vintage store in Denver, where they carried all his favorite band T-shirts from the '80s. Bloomingdale's wasn't really his scene.

Elijah noticed Steffan awkwardly examining the women's jackets around him.

"Dude, I think I saw a sign for the electronics department. Want to head over with me?" he said.

"Meet us by the main entrance in thirty minutes!" called Chloe to their retreating backs.

"Now! Lip glosses. Who wants to try on all of them with me?" Eva asked the other girls, grinning.

Chapter 4
An Impromptu Performance

Steffan's visit to Strawberry Fields was saved for last so that the KIDZ BOP Kids could spend some time wandering around Central Park and seeing the sights.

"This is Central Park," Eva sighed, spreading her hands out over her head to indicate the vastness of the park. "It's the most amazing place on Earth."

"There are horses!" said Charisma, examining a map at the park entrance.

"Yes!" said Eva. "We should go riding one of these days. I've never ridden a horse."

"Ooooh, you must! It's the best experience in the world!" said Charisma. She thought about her beloved horse, Carrot, in the stables back home. She hoped her dad was giving Carrot lots of love and attention while she was gone.

Strawberry Fields was as peaceful and serene as Steffan could ever hope. In the center of the small area lay the large, round mosaic pathway that made Strawberry Fields famous. The mosaics spelled out the word "Imagine" in the middle of the circle, after one of John Lennon's most famous (and one of Steffan's favorite) songs. Steffan had insisted on a special trip back to the hotel for his guitar. He couldn't visit John Lennon's memorial empty-handed.

Now, he sat down on the ground near the word "Imagine" and started strumming his guitar. It seemed inappropriate to play one of John Lennon's own songs when no one could ever beat his performances of them. So, Steffan played something he wrote. It was a song called "Magic."

The other KIDZ BOP Kids had seen Steffan's audition video posted online. They knew he was talented. But until that moment, they had no idea how talented their friend was.

"Whoa!" Hanna muttered under her breath. She already knew that Steffan and his guitar were practically inseparable, but watching Steffan play was a new experience. Hanna had never seen anyone play the guitar like it was just an extension of his arm. Steffan made it all look so easy.

When the song was over, the KIDZ BOP Kids and Chloe clapped. Some other tourists who were standing around clapped as well.

"Hey!" said one bystander. "Do you know any John Mayer?"

Steffan smiled and began to play "Waiting on the World to Change." It seemed like a fitting song for that moment, one that the peace-loving John Lennon himself might appreciate.

Soon, a small crowd of people had gathered around to listen. When one song ended, someone would shout a request, and Steffan would play it. If he didn't know the words, one of the other KIDZ BOP Kids would start singing along. Soon, they were all singing along with every song.

As the impromptu concert went on, a man sitting on a bench near Steffan got his violin out of a case near his feet and began to play with the melody. A man holding a bucket drum sitting nearby began to tap out the beat. Elijah began to move to the music. It had been way too long since he'd been able to dance. Soon, he was trying out some new dance moves. Charisma joined him, throwing in some gymnastics from her years of cheerleading. Elijah watched, impressed.

A woman carrying a saxophone joined in, playing along with Steffan and the other musicians. More and more people gathered around to listen. And as Steffan continued to play, they shouted out song requests.

Hanna dug her camcorder out of her backpack and began to film the show. She wanted to upload it onto her video blog. She wanted to record everything for her friends back home to see.

"I think Steffan may know every song ever written," said Eva to Hanna.

"I know! Cute and talented!" Hanna replied, slowly panning over the crowd of onlookers.

It was starting to get dark when the KIDZ BOP Kids and Chloe finally left Central Park.

"You are all wonderful performers. I can't wait until I get all of you into rehearsal tomorrow," said Chloe with a grin. "But first, I think it's time to head back to the hotel and order some room service. I don't know about you guys, but I need a cheeseburger."

"Now you're talking, Chloe," said Elijah.

"Take a look at this room service menu!" Elijah called. "You can order an ice cream sundae with anything on it, and they'll bring it to you. I think I'm in heaven!"

"I'm ordering a big plate of French fries just for me," said Hanna.

"Pizza! With artichokes!" said Eva.

"What? You New Yorkers and your fancy food," said Charisma with a teasing grin. "I want my pizza with pepperoni. Hold the artichokes."

"If you tried it, you might like it," said Eva, raising an eyebrow.

"I'll try it," said Steffan. "Along with these nachos." He pointed to the menu.

Eva laughed.

"What? I'm starving!" said Steffan.

"I'll order room service!" Chloe announced. "You guys get into the living room and fire up the Wii. I'm in the mood for some *KIDZ BOP Dance Party*!"

"I smell a challenge!" said Elijah.

"I hope you brought your A-game, buddy," said Chloe.

"Ohhhh, it's on!" said Elijah. "I'm gonna go warm up."

Thirty minutes later, a hotel waiter pushed a gleaming cart of food through the door of the KIDZ BOP suite. As soon as he was gone, the kids sat around the table with trays of food and had a feast like none of them had ever seen.

"I can't dance on a full stomach," said Chloe. "But just know that this dance tournament is not over."

Elijah just grinned.

"This is like Thanksgiving without the disgusting yams!" Hanna exclaimed, dipping a fry in ketchup.

"Yams! Gross," said Charisma. "You should come to my house for Thanksgiving. No yams and *three kinds* of pie."

"I'm in," said Steffan. "Seriously."

"Not me," Elijah said. "There is no way I'm missing my mom's sweet potato pie. All of your pies won't make up for one of hers."

Eva took a bite of her artichoke pizza and thought about Thanksgiving. Her parents had been away on Thanksgiving for the last two years. Her dad was in Milan, and her mom was in Japan for a fashion shoot. They'd certainly never cooked a dinner as a family.

"I'm in too!" she said, smiling at Charisma.

Just yesterday, the KIDZ BOP Kids were strangers from all over the United States. And now, they were all in the hotel room that would be their home for the next several weeks—at least until after the concert with Madison Day! And then who knew what would happen next?

"Let's watch a movie," said Hanna.

"What should we watch?" asked Steffan.

"Oh! How about the new *Transformers* movie?" said Charisma. "I have it in my suitcase!"

"Sweet!" said Elijah, "I haven't seen it yet. Bring it on."

Charisma ran to her suitcase and came back with the video.

The kids settled into their chairs and prepared to watch the movie.

"After this," said Elijah in his best Christian Bale Batman voice, "We are watching *Batman*."

Chapter 5
Lights! Camera! Rehearse!

The next morning, the KIDZ BOP Kids took the subway downtown. Chloe knew the owner of an old theater "with amazing acoustics" where they would begin putting their songs and choreography together. Today, they would begin rehearsing the choreography for the Madison Day show.

Steffan had felt weird leaving his guitar back in the hotel suite. He rarely went anywhere without it. Not holding a guitar gave Steffan the freedom to dance, but he couldn't escape the strange way it made him feel to perform without his trusty guitar in his hands.

"How did this Madison Day thing happen anyway?" asked Hanna, sitting down on the stage to tie up her dance shoes. "It's not like we're famous yet. How do we get to open for Madison Day? She's a superstar."

"Chloe told me that she knows Madison Day personally," said Eva.

"*What?*" Charisma squeaked.

"But how did Chloe convince Madison to let us open for her?" Charisma asked.

"I don't know," said Eva. "I—"

Chloe herself had entered the stage, breaking Eva off midsentence. She was dressed in leggings and a tank top and had her hair pulled back in a tight bun. She did not smile at the kids. The Chloe from yesterday was their fun-loving manager. Today, she was Chloe Malone, a top Broadway choreographer.

"We have a lot of work to do, KIDZ BOP Kids," Chloe said. "Are you ready to work hard?"

"Yep," said Elijah.

"I can't hear you," Chloe said.

"I said '*yes*,'" Elijah replied.

"What about the rest of you? Are you ready to work hard?"

"*Yes!*" the KIDZ BOP Kids shouted in unison.

"Great," said Chloe. "You guys will be performing twelve songs when you open for Madison Day. We have six weeks to learn the songs and the choreography. And it must be flawless. But you're going to work hard, and by the time that concert rolls around, you will know these songs and the choreography so well that it will be as natural to you as breathing."

She continued, "I'm going to tell you that there will be several vocal and dance solos throughout the concert. And I will pick the top dancer for each of them. So, if you want to stand out, you will have to work hard. I won't be giving you anything you don't earn."

Eva stood up a little straighter at that comment. She was a strong dancer, but after seeing Elijah and Charisma dance in the park yesterday, she felt like a klutz in comparison. How would she ever land one of the dance solos with competition like that? She glanced over at Hanna, who had a similar expression of worry on her face.

"Well, if you're ready to learn the choreography for our first song, then line up in this order," said Chloe. "Steffan, Charisma, Hanna, Elijah, Eva." She pointed to the places on the floor where she wanted them to stand. The KIDZ BOP Kids lined up and got ready to dance.

"Whew! I'm exhausted!" said Elijah, not looking the least bit exhausted, as he flopped down on the stage.

Eva, on the other hand, felt like she had been hit by a cross-town bus. After two hours of rehearsal, she felt like collapsing in the middle of the floor.

"Take a ten-minute break, kids!" Chloe called. She hadn't broken a sweat during the entire rehearsal despite the fact she never stopped moving.

Hanna sat down on the floor near Eva and took a big drink from her water bottle.

"I can't keep up!" she said.

"Me neither," said Eva.

Charisma plopped down next to them.

"Isn't this great?" she said. "I haven't danced this hard since our last cheer competition."

"Yeah!" said Eva. "You'll have to show me how to do a back flip like that."

"Oh, totally!" said Charisma. "We can work on it now if you want."

"Uh . . ." said Eva, rubbing her sore feet. "Maybe during the next break."

"Up!" Chloe called a few minutes later. "We have to get back to rehearsal!"

Elijah leaped right up from where he was sitting on the floor and got into place. Once again, Eva wondered how she would ever be able to keep up with him.

Elijah was chosen for the first dance solo. Everyone knew it was going to happen before Chloe even announced it. While the other KIDZ BOP Kids struggled to pick up the choreography, at least at first, Elijah was moving along to Chloe's moves perfectly. He made dancing look so easy.

"Elijah, stop free-styling until everyone knows the choreography!" Chloe called.

Elijah had started adding extra kicks and jumps to the song.

Eva rolled her eyes at him. "Show-off!" she said.

Elijah flashed her a toothy grin.

"You were slow on that turn, Hanna!" Chloe called.

"Sorry!" Hanna said and struggled to catch up with her friends. She hoped that she would be able to better prove herself when they started adding the vocals to their performance.

"Okay!" Chloe said, "Let's stop for a minute. Elijah, you'll be taking the first dance solo for 'Dynamite.' Congratulations."

"Woo!" Elijah shouted. Steffan smiled and gave him a high-five.

"Well-deserved," Steffan said, and he meant it. Before rehearsal, Elijah had told him how much he wanted that solo.

"Let's move on to the next song for now, shall we?" Chloe said. She pushed "play" on her iPod and Katy Perry's "Firework" began to play.

"Follow along, and try to keep up!" Chloe said, "And five, six, seven, eight!"

Elijah was having the time of his life. He had spent the whole day doing what he loved best—dancing—and he got picked for the first dance solo! Just wait until Madison Day (and the fans!) caught a load of his moves.

But the highlight of the first day of rehearsal for Elijah was watching Eva's reaction when she found that he had added Kool-Aid powder to her water bottle, turning it bright red.

"What is this?" said Eva loudly.

Elijah burst into laughter. He couldn't help it. He'd been carrying that Kool-Aid packet around all day, waiting for just the right moment. When Eva set her water down and turned her back on it for just a moment, Elijah knew it was time. There was nothing like a well-played prank.

After rehearsal, the exhausted KIDZ BOP Kids grabbed their gear and headed back uptown to the hotel. It had already started to get dark outside. They had spent the whole day in rehearsal!

"I think we should order a New York–style pizza and play some more *KIDZ BOP Dance Party*!" Elijah said as they walked into the suite.

"Oh," said Hanna. "Eva and I need to do some practicing before tomorrow morning."

Elijah's face fell. "Aw, come on, you guys! How could you say no to a dance party?"

"I have to if I want one of those dance solos before you take them all!" said Hanna.

Chapter 6
And the Solo Goes to . . .

Early the next morning, the KIDZ BOP Kids and Chloe launched right into vocal practice.

Each song would have several vocal solos, and as with the dance solos, each KIDZ BOP Kid would have to sing his or her best to land one. And Chloe was not going to make it easy for them. She wanted the best of the best.

Hanna looked at the song sheet. "Oh, there's a big solo in 'Naturally'!" she cried.

"I know!" said Charisma, looking over her shoulder at the list. "I love that song. Are you going to try out for the solo?"

Hanna nodded and tried to be calm. She didn't want to jinx her chances of landing the solo. This was the song Hanna had performed in her audition video. Selena Gomez was Hanna's number-one favorite singer and actress of *all time*. Hanna knew the song backwards and forwards, and no one could out-perform her singing the solo.

She noticed Eva looking at the copy of the list as well and carefully writing things down in her notebook. Eva, being completely organized, was no doubt writing down the list of solos she wanted.

"Let's get started," Chloe called, clapping her hands to get their attention. "We'll run through each song twice, and then I'll ask who wants to try out for the solos," said Chloe.

The KIDZ BOP Kids lined up to start working on the first song. No one was remotely surprised when the first solo went to Steffan. They'd all heard him play an acoustic version on his guitar a few days before. When Chloe asked them to raise their hands to vote for Steffan for the solo, everyone's hands shot up, even Charisma's—and she had also auditioned for the solo.

"Naturally" was next on the list. As they sang through the song the first time, Hanna's hands started to shake. She had an opportunity to prove herself, and she just couldn't mess up.

When Chloe asked who wanted to try out for the solo, Hanna's and Eva's hands both shot up in the air. Eva gave Hanna a tiny smile and a shrug that said, "Sorry, but I want it too." Hanna frowned. Eva knew how much she loved Selena Gomez. What was she trying to prove by trying for the solo too? Well, Hanna was just going to have to work twice as hard.

"Okay, then," said Chloe. "Let's take it from the top. Eva, you go first, and then we'll go through it again and Hanna can take the solo. Then, we'll take a vote."

Chloe pushed "play" on the iPod, and the familiar beats of Hanna's favorite song began to play. Listening to Eva sing the solo was disheartening to Hanna. Eva was such a talented singer! Hanna saw her solo slowly slipping away. "Wait a second," Hanna thought. "It's not over 'til it's over. Just do your best."

When it came time for Hanna to do the solo, she sang her heart out. And at the end of it, she felt completely confident.

But the solo went to Eva anyway. When the other KIDZ BOP Kids' hands shot up in the air, voting for Eva, Hanna just nodded and got back in place.

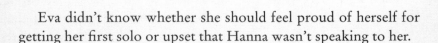

Eva didn't know whether she should feel proud of herself for getting her first solo or upset that Hanna wasn't speaking to her.

Hanna had muttered, "Congratulations," to Eva and tried to smile, but when rehearsal resumed, she wouldn't even look at her. "What's the big deal?" Eva thought to herself. "It's not like being Selena Gomez's number one fan gave Hanna more of a right to sing the solo than anyone else."

"Okay, let's run through the song with the choreography!" said Chloe.

The KIDZ BOP Kids lined up, and Chloe began to play the song. After a minute, she stopped the music and looked around at the KIDZ BOP Kids.

"You're falling behind, Hanna. And, Eva, you look like this is the worst thing you've had to do all day. What's going on?" asked Chloe.

Both girls shrugged.

"Well, I want to see smiles. I want to see *enthusiasm*," said Chloe. "This is the big time!"

She started the music again and watched them dance for a minute before stopping them again.

"Elijah," said Chloe. "This isn't Elijah and the KIDZ BOP Kids. This is just the KIDZ BOP Kids. And you're part of that group. So, stick with the others and dance to the choreography I have provided to you."

Elijah frowned. He had been throwing in a bit of his own style here and there to see if Chloe would notice. Obviously, she had, but without the positive outcome Elijah had expected.

"Let's continue," Chloe said.

An hour later, the KIDZ BOP Kids were sprawled on the stage floor, drinking bottles of water and trying to catch a few minutes of rest time. Even Elijah, who was usually tireless, looked exhausted. Chloe, who still hadn't broken a sweat or sat down even once, walked among them, handing out the sheet music for the next song.

"There's something I'm not seeing here, KIDZ BOP Kids, and that's a sense of group dynamic," she said. "Remember, you are a group, and you have to work together as one. So, Elijah, that means if someone misses a step, it's your job to help him or her get back on track. Eva, if one of your friends forgets the lyrics, it's your job to remind him or her what they are. Every single person here is a part of the team, and we have to play like a team."

"You sound like my basketball coach," said Elijah.

"I am your coach," said Chloe. "Don't forget that I have the power to bench you." She smiled, raising an eyebrow at Elijah.

"Back to practice," said Chloe simply. They had a lot of work to do before the day was over.

"Right, Coach!" said Elijah.

Chapter 7
Elijah the Prankster Strikes Again!

Rehearsal the next day was as long and tiring as the one the day before. All of the KIDZ BOP Kids were in bed and asleep by 9 P.M. Eva fell asleep before they even had dinner and woke in the middle of the night starving and wondering when it got dark outside. By the time the fourth day of rehearsal rolled around, everyone had a few vocal and dance solos, but they were far too busy to enjoy their success. Chloe reassured them that soon their bodies would adjust to the length of rehearsals and they would stop being so tired. But at the end of the fourth day, everyone had stopped believing her.

Charisma was flat-out exhausted. She hadn't felt so tired since her gymnastics team took it upon themselves to practice until midnight one night before they headed to state finals. That same week, she had been writing a paper on *Great Expectations* and working on her campaign for class president. So, at the end of it, when her mom picked her up from that late-night practice, she broke down into tears from the stress of it all.

Charisma was thinking about that time as she sprang into her dance solo for "The Only Exception," a solo she had worked hard for, and promptly forgot the choreography. It was like her brain completely shut down, and all she could think about was taking a nap. They'd run through so many songs that day, that Charisma realized she didn't know where one song ended and the next began. She stopped dancing and stood there for a moment, and then burst into tears.

"Okay," said Chloe, turning off the music and patting her on the back. "Just go sit down for a minute." She looked around. "Does anyone else here need a break?"

All of the KIDZ BOP Kids nodded.

"Then, let's take five," said Chloe.

Hanna sat as far as she could from Eva, who looked annoyed about it. The two were still not really talking. Steffan sat down on the edge of stage and didn't really talk to or look at anyone.

Charisma sat still wiping away tears. No one was used to seeing her that way. Normally, Charisma was the queen of enthusiasm and the one who kept them all going with her pep talks.

"Hey, Charisma," whispered Elijah as he sat down next to her. "You know what might cheer you up?"

"What?" she asked.

"A whoopee cushion," Elijah replied.

Chloe rarely sat down during a rehearsal, but when she did, she sat on the bench of the upright piano near the stage. Elijah had been carefully watching Chloe for the last few days, and so that morning when he arrived at rehearsal, he placed a filled whoopee cushion under the lid of the bench and left it to see how long Chloe would go before sitting down. As Chloe went to sit down on the bench, Elijah moved next to Charisma to watch the show.

"PHHHHHHPPPPPPPPPPBBBBBBBBBBBBBBBTT!"

"*Elijah!*" Chloe shouted, pulling the whoopee cushion from the bench and glaring at him.

Elijah had expected everyone to burst out laughing, but his prank had quite the opposite effect. Everyone was too tired to see the humor in anything at that moment.

"What is wrong with you?" asked Eva, glaring at him. "Chloe is our manager. You don't go playing rude pranks on her."

"Come on!" said Elijah. "It was funny."

"It's fine, Eva," said Chloe, reassuringly. She actually found Elijah's prank kind of funny. Of course, she couldn't tell him that, or he might try it again.

But Eva continued to glare. She had had quite enough of Elijah's pranks over the last few days. The day before, he'd shoved two hamburger buns (that he'd craftily gotten from room service at the hotel) into the toes of Steffan's shoes and watched in delight as Steffan tried to put them on, only to find that overnight his shoes had mysteriously gotten smaller.

Elijah looked over at Steffan to see what he thought of the latest prank, and Steffan was gone. He'd climbed down from the stage and went to sit out in the darkened auditorium, away from the others.

Maybe Eva was right. Maybe he was taking this pranking thing too far.

Chloe looked around at the group in dismay. They had less than a month and a half to rehearse before the Madison Square Garden show, and most of the KIDZ BOP Kids weren't on speaking terms. She sighed. Chloe had worked with a lot of exhausted dancers in her day, but this was a mess.

"We have weeks, kids! Weeks! And then, we open for Madison Day!" she said. "We can't rehearse with all of you sitting around like lumps being grumpy. Up! Up!"

She waved her hands in the air in a lifting motion. None of the kids moved.

"Well, I don't know what to do," said Chloe. "All I've tried to do is get you all to work together. I know you're tired, but we have to keep going."

Elijah looked up at her from where he was sitting. He knew what he had to do; the same thing he did when people on his basketball team got upset after a loss: make them laugh.

Elijah stood up and walked over to the piano bench where Chloe had left his whoopee cushion. He blew it up, set it on the chair next to Charisma, and nonchalantly and very slowly sat down on it.

Pppppppppbbbbbbbbbbbbbbbtttttttttt!"

"Excuse me," Elijah said, not cracking a smile.

There was a silence all across the theater.

Charisma was the first to start giggling. And then Eva. And then Hanna caught the giggles as well. Even Chloe was smirking. And somewhere out in the darkness of the auditorium, Steffan let out a guffaw.

"Give me that," said Charisma, and she grabbed the whoopee cushion. She blew it up and sat down on it so that the air leaked out in a staccato, like machine gun fire.

"*Aaaaaaa*!" said Eva, and fell over on the stage where she was sitting and started to laugh.

Elijah took the whoopee cushion back, blew it up, put it under his left armpit, and squeezed it under his arm.

At this, even Chloe had to sit back down on her bench and laugh with her head in her hands.

When they had finally all recovered, Chloe said, "What do you guys say we call it a day?" And that was the first time they had agreed all day.

Chapter 8
Burgers, Beads, and BFFs

Eva sat on her bed, carefully stringing together a long set of beads. In her spare time, Eva liked to design jewelry using beads she found at vintage and antique stores. Her latest creation was of the deepest blue, made from some costume jewelry she'd found. Since rehearsal had started, she'd barely had time for her hobby. But something about the way rehearsal had ended made her feel energized again. And she wanted to finish this particular necklace before the concert.

Eva looked up to see Hanna enter the room and quickly looked back down. Hanna had been giving her the cold shoulder for days. There was no sense in trying to be friendly now.

"Eva, I'm sorry," Hanna suddenly blurted out. Eva looked up to see an expression of surprise on Hanna's face, as if the apology fell out accidentally.

Hanna continued, "I was just being selfish. But you deserved the solo, and I want you to have it." She sat down on Eva's bed beside her friend and finally looked her in the eyes for the first time in days.

"I'm sorry, too," said Eva. "I knew you wanted the solo, and I should have told you I was going to try for it as well beforehand."

"So . . . friends again?" Hanna said shyly, putting her hand out to shake.

Eva ignored the hand and grabbed her friend in a big hug.

"Friends," she said.

Suddenly, Charisma appeared in the doorway. "Aw, did you two finally make up?" she asked.

Hanna and Eva laughed.

"Actually, I'm glad you're both here," said Eva. "I wanted to give you something." She opened the box where she kept her beads and pulled out two necklaces, one a shiny sea green and the other of the palest pink. She handed the green one to Charisma and the pink one to Hanna. Their favorite colors!

"And this one is mine," Eva said, showing them the blue one. "I thought we could all wear them for the big concert. You know, for luck?"

At 7 A.M. the next morning, the KIDZ BOP Kids were all up and dressed in their dance gear and ready to head to rehearsal. Elijah had even made slices of toast for everyone and filled all their water bottles. (No Kool-Aid. Just water, this time.)

"What's going on with you guys?" Chloe asked, warily, looking from face to face for a sign that they were playing some kind of elaborate practical joke on her.

"Nothing," said Elijah, raising an eyebrow in a very Chloe-like fashion and imitating her voice to perfection. "We just want to get going as soon as possible today. There's lots to do before the concert, you know."

Chloe shook her head and rolled her eyes. "Let me get my bag," she said.

Rehearsal for the next several days was a whole new experience for the KIDZ BOP Kids. For the first time, they felt like opening for Madison Day at Madison Square Garden in just a few weeks was entirely possible. When Eva fell behind on the choreography, Elijah caught her eye and showed her the right steps. When Steffan missed his solo in "Cooler Than Me," Charisma sang the words for him until he caught on. They went through all of the songs with the choreography before it was even noon, and what mistakes they made were quickly corrected. The KIDZ BOP Kids had learned to help each other out.

"I'm so proud of you guys!" Chloe gushed. "This show is really coming together."

"Does that mean no more rehearsal for today?" Elijah teased.

"No, we still have to rehearse," Chloe laughed, "But I am going to take you all out to lunch to celebrate."

For lunch, the KIDZ BOP Kids settled on Burger Joint, a trendy little burger place hidden in the corner of a fancy midtown hotel lobby.

"Famous people go there!" Eva insisted. "We might see someone super cool!"

After they ordered their burgers, fries, and shakes and settled into their tiny wooden booth, the KIDZ BOP Kids looked around eagerly for celebrities. But, as it was only two o'clock in the afternoon, there weren't many people at all hanging around the popular burger place, much less famous people.

There was a group of teenagers hanging out in a corner booth, and a family with three kids waiting at the counter for their order.

"This place is cool," said Charisma looking around. Despite being in the lobby of Le Parker Meridien, Burger Joint was a very unassuming place. The walls were wooden and covered with graffiti. Even the menu was written in marker on a piece of cardboard.

"The graffiti is celebrity signatures," said Eva. "See, Hanna. Selena Gomez signed right there." She pointed at a small blue signature on the wall.

"Whoa!" Hanna exclaimed, looking around wildly as if Selena Gomez herself was in the room.

"Down, Hanna!" Steffan teased. He was grinning as he looked around for signatures of his favorite bands.

"*Beyoncé!*" Elijah exclaimed, pointing to a signature high on one wall. "And Jay-Z signed right next to her!"

The KIDZ BOP Kids all looked around to see the signatures.

Charisma was looking around eagerly to see if Madison Day had signed the wall anywhere when she noticed a girl staring at them from the booth where she was sitting. She was probably ten years old, and wore an "I <3 New York!" T-shirt. When she saw Charisma looking back at her, she glanced quickly back down at her burger.

"Hey, pass me the ketchup," said Elijah. It was sitting next to Charisma's elbow; she passed it to him.

"Hi."

The KIDZ BOP Kids looked up to see the girl from the other table standing next to theirs smiling shyly.

"I'm Erin," she said. Whispering, she added, "I know you're the KIDZ BOP Kids."

"How did you know who we were?" Eva asked, feeling flattered.

"I saw you guys on the KIDZ BOP website!" said Erin, a big smile growing on her face. "All of my friends know who you are."

The KIDZ BOP Kids introduced themselves and signed autographs for Erin. It felt strange, signing their names for someone. Their first real fan!

"I wish I could be at your concert," she said. "But I live in Utah."

"Not to worry," Chloe had said, "The KIDZ BOP Kids will be going out on tour soon. We'll probably have shows in Salt Lake City, so we'll see you then!"

Erin went back to her own table grinning from ear to ear. When her family got up to leave, she waved goodbye.

"Someday," Elijah predicted, "I hope our names will be written on the wall of Burger Joint."

Back at the theater, the KIDZ BOP Kids went through the show again. This time, nobody missed a cue. Rather than being nervous and tired as they had been for the first week of rehearsal, the KIDZ BOP Kids were starting to get a feeling of excitement that permeated the whole theater. And it was easy to understand why. In the very near future, they would be opening for Madison Day!

PART 2

Chapter 9
Here Comes Trouble

After an amazing rehearsal the day before, Chloe decided to give the KIDZ BOP Kids the next morning off, so they were walking up to Central Park to have a relaxing morning outdoors.

"What is that glowing orb in the sky?" Elijah joked, shielding his eyes from the sun. It had been days since he'd been able to spend any time outdoors during the day.

"I don't . . . know," Eva replied. Since their blow-out at rehearsal several days before, the two were getting along, even joking around together.

"Who's in for a game of basketball when we get there?" Elijah asked. He hadn't played since his last morning back home in Detroit!

"Count me in," said Steffan. What he secretly longed for was a kayak and a nice stretch of Colorado River, but basketball would have to do for now.

Hanna, Eva, and Charisma carried along a blanket to stretch out on the grass and lie on.

"I am *dying* to get back to my Twilight book," said Hanna, hugging her book to her chest. "Just when it started getting good, we had rehearsal every day."

Charisma just wanted put on her sunglasses, paint her nails, and write a few pages in her diary.

Eva carried along the latest issue of *Vogue* magazine.

The girls stretched out their blanket on the grass near the basketball courts, while Steffan and Elijah headed over to join one of the games. It was one of those bright and sunny days that made Eva crave ice cream. She pulled her Ralph Lauren fedora down over her forehead to block out the sun and began to read.

"Hey, guys. Need some extra players?" asked Elijah, as he and Steffan entered one of the courts. There were two kids about their age shooting baskets. Might as well try and make some new friends! One-on-one just wasn't as much fun.

"Sure!" said one of the kids. "I'm Chris. This is Derek." He pointed to his friend.

"Cool," said Elijah. "This is Steffan, and I'm Elijah."

The boys shook hands all around. They split into teams, and the game was on.

It had been far too long since Elijah had last played. But all of the dance rehearsal he had done in the last week had just made him stronger. As he stole the ball, dribbled down the court, and made the first point, he felt like he could take on the New York Knicks, no problem!

Chris, who was much taller, blocked Elijah with his arm, and Elijah just dribbled around him and made for the basket again. He was used to playing with taller opponents. Steffan, who was on the opposing team, knocked the ball out of his hands.

"You won't have that ball for long!" Elijah teased his friend.

"We'll see about that," Steffan said and shot the ball right over Elijah's head and into the basket.

"You *do* have some moves! You've been holding out on me!" said Elijah.

"I was basketball team captain two years running," said Steffan with a shrug.

Elijah shook his head. There were so many things he didn't know about Steffan. Who knew he was a whiz at basketball?

"The score is tied," said Chris, giving Steffan a high-five.

Elijah was going to have to get out his best moves if his team was going to win. Derek tossed him the ball.

"Watch this," he said to his teammate, and he shot past Steffan and dribbled toward the basket. Elijah leaped into the air and shot the ball toward the basket, just like he had done playing his dad a million times. *Swish!*

But when Elijah hit the ground again, something went terribly wrong. Normally, he tucked himself into a crouch to keep the pressure off his knees. But, when he landed, his foot turned at a strange angle. He felt a sharp pain in his ankle as his feet hit the ground, like something snapped.

"*Ow!*" Elijah shouted and sat down hard on the concrete basketball court.

"Whoa, man! Are you okay?" asked Steffan running to his side.

"I don't know," said Elijah.

"Try to stand up," said Chris, offering him a hand.

Elijah got to his feet.

"Aaaaa!" he said, hopping on his uninjured leg. The pain was pretty intense.

"I'm calling Chloe," Steffan said, pulling out his cell phone. "We need to get you to the emergency room."

The KIDZ BOP Kids and Chloe were sitting in the hospital waiting room. Afternoon rehearsal was canceled. Everyone wore a similar expression of worry on their face.

Elijah's parents had hopped the first plane to New York, and now they were back in Elijah's hospital room talking to a doctor about his injuries. The EMT had said it wasn't broken, but according to Chloe there were worse things than broken bones. A torn ligament or an injured tendon had left many a dancer in one of her Broadway shows laid up for months.

Suddenly one of the nurses who had been taking care of Elijah entered the waiting room.

"Are you Elijah's friends?" he asked. "He wants to see you."

The KIDZ BOP Kids trooped back through the hospital corridors to Elijah's room.

Elijah was sitting on the bed, his foot propped up on a pillow in the middle of the bed. The expression on his face was one of total disgust, as he looked down at his bandaged ankle.

"Elijah!" Charisma said, rushing to his bedside. "How is it?"

Elijah's dad answered for him.

"It's a severe sprain, kids. Elijah won't be dancing for a while."

At least that explained the look on Elijah's face.

"It gets worse," Elijah said, looking around at his friends. "Mom and Dad are taking me back to Detriot tonight."

"What? Why?" Hanna cried.

"We have a doctor who specializes in this type of injury," said Elijah's mom. "We want him to look at Elijah's ankle."

"Will he be back in time for the concert?" Steffan asked, glancing up at Elijah's dad.

"The doctor said no dancing for a month," Elijah's dad replied.

"What about the show?" Charisma whispered so that only Chloe could hear her.

"I don't know," Chloe replied.

Chapter 10
A Secret KIDZ BOP Mission

Early the next morning when the KIDZ BOP Kids would normally be rehearsing, Elijah was on his way to Detriot. Madison Day was going to have to find a new opening act for her Madison Square Garden performance. The KIDZ BOP Kids were not going to be able to do it. How could they with one of their best dancers recovering from an injury?

Chloe had spent most of the morning locked in her room in the suite on the phone with Madison Day's manager trying to explain the situation to her.

"Well, it's been real, you guys," said Eva. "I've really loved the time we've had, but I guess it's over."

"At least I can cheer at the football game on Friday," said Charisma, brightly. She had been trying to find the positive in the situation since they first learned that Elijah would not be returning from the hospital. And she really did miss the members of her squad. Maybe it was okay for her to head back to California and just resume the normal life she had led before.

"Getting back to Colorado will be nice," said Steffan, unconvincingly. "I could use a day of rock climbing."

Hanna looked around at the sad faces of her friends. What could she do? She hated to feel this way, but it was worse to know that your friends were feeling the same way.

"Well," she said suddenly, "I'm not going to sit here and mope. Steffan, why don't you sing us a song?"

"Sure," said Steffan, giving her a weak smile. Hanna was right. Why were they just sitting around being miserable? This might be their last chance to perform together before they all went back home.

"Oh, play that one you were working on the other night!" said Charisma.

"That song isn't done. I was just messing around," said Steffan, smoothing his hair away from his eyes.

Charisma shrugged. "I liked it," she said.

"You've never been shy about playing for us before, Steffan. Play it!" said Eva.

Steffan went to his bedroom and got out his guitar. The room seemed very empty without Elijah's belongings. He brought the guitar back to the living room where Eva, Hanna, and Charisma were sitting. He began to play.

Steffan's voice was like a salve on a wound. As soon as he began to sing, the troubles shared by the remaining four KIDZ BOP Kids melted away.

Soon, Hanna, Charisma, and Eva had picked up the lyrics and were singing along. When that song ended, Steffan played an acoustic version of "Just a Dream." The main dance solo in their version of the song had belonged to Elijah. The first time they'd seen it, all of them stopped dancing to watch.

"Awesome!" said Charisma, jumping from her chair and dancing along to the song. Before too long, they were all laughing and had forgotten their worries altogether. Hanna looked around at her friends and realized how good they were, even without Elijah.

"I don't understand why we can't go ahead and do the Madison Day show," she said, suddenly sitting up straighter in her chair.

"What?" asked Eva.

Steffan stopped playing, and Charisma stopped dancing.

"I mean," said Hanna, "there has to be a way for us to do the concert, even without Elijah."

"We can't," said Eva. "Chloe would have to rewrite the choreography for only four people. We only have a few weeks."

"I might have an idea," said Hanna.

"What you're asking for cannot be done," said Chloe. "First of all, we have weeks to put this thing together, not months. Secondly, we are on a strict rehearsal schedule. This would require a lot more rehearsal than you already do. . . ." Chloe ticked off the reasons why they couldn't find a new KIDZ BOP Kid to replace Elijah for the concert one by one on her fingers.

"Thirdly," she continued, "It took a *week* for you to all learn how to work together! I do not think I can handle throwing a new member into the mix and having to go through that again!"

"Chloe, we are willing to do whatever we need to do to make this show happen," said Hanna. "Eva, Charisma, Steffan, and I talked about it, and we will work twice as hard in rehearsal."

"And just where are we supposed to find a new KIDZ BOP Kid at this point?" Chloe asked.

"We talked about that," said Steffan, "We're already heading out on the KIDZ BOP promotional tour next week. Why not extend our stays in those cities and give kids there a chance to audition? We find a new person, and he or she joins us in New York to begin rehearsals. We know the show. The challenge is adding the new member and helping him learn it."

"I don't think a new person would have time to learn the choreography," said Chloe, wearily.

"Look how fast Elijah learned the choreography! He knew all of it within a few days," said Charisma. "If we found the right person, someone as talented as Elijah, we could pull this off."

"As your manager, I'm still voting no, KIDZ BOP Kids," said Chloe. "Now, go pack up your belongings. I need to call your parents now and see about getting all of you home."

Disheartened, Eva went back to the room she shared with Charisma and Hanna and started putting her belongings back in her suitcase. It was no problem for her parents to run downtown in a cab and pick her up. She could be in her own bed by tonight if she really wanted to. The problem was, she really didn't want to. But Chloe seemed adamant. The concert was not going to happen.

"What are you doing?" said Hanna, suddenly entering the room.

"Packing up my stuff," said Eva.

"Well, stop it!" said Hanna. "This isn't over until we say it is. Don't give up hope just yet!"

"What could we possibly do now to save the show?" Eva asked, skeptically.

"I have a plan!" said Charisma, entering the room behind Hanna. "But all four of us have to help out if we're going to convince Chloe."

Eva set down the socks she was preparing to pack and looked up at her friends.

"What's the plan?" she asked.

"Get your dance clothes on and meet us in the hallway in ten minutes," said Charisma quietly. "And whatever you do, don't let Chloe see you!"

Fifteen minutes later, Eva, Hanna, Charisma, and Steffan were in a cab heading downtown.

"Do you have the keys, Steffan?" Hanna asked again.

"Yup," Steffan replied again. Hanna had already checked three times. He had the keys to the theater gripped tightly in his hand. Charisma had been the one to take them off the table before they left the hotel suite.

"And the note?" Hanna asked.

"I left it right where Chloe would see it," said Charisma with a grin. This was exciting! She felt like a spy on a secret mission.

The note had said, "Meet us at the theater at 8 P.M. Don't be late!—Charisma, Steffan, Hanna, and Eva."

There wasn't a question in any of their minds. Chloe would be there.

Chapter 11
On the Road

Charisma found the stage lights and turned them on. Eva hooked her iPod up to the speakers and tested the sound on the microphones, and Hanna opened and closed the stage curtains to make sure they were working correctly.

Nothing could go wrong tonight! They had to convince Chloe to let them do the Madison Day show. And if the only way to do that was to put on a surprise performance for her, so be it.

Steffan had positioned himself by the front door of the theater to keep an eye out for Chloe. She wasn't due to arrive until 8, but if she showed up early, mad that the KIDZ BOP Kids had taken her keys or left the hotel without telling her, they had to be prepared.

"Should we try to practice a little before she arrives?" Eva asked, clicking through the playlist to make sure it was in the right order.

"There's no time," Hanna replied. "We'll just have to rely on the practice we've already had."

"I believe in us!" Charisma exclaimed.

At 7:55, the four remaining KIDZ BOP Kids gathered backstage and prepared for the performance.

"What if Chloe didn't see the note?" Eva whispered.

"She did," said Hanna, nodding. She wasn't actually sure, but Hanna wasn't about to admit that to her friends.

After a few moments, the silence of the theater was broken by the sound of a door opening and closing. They heard footsteps walking down the aisle.

"Well? I'm here!" they heard Chloe say. "What's this all about?"

"Take a seat!" called Hanna in reply.

"Anywhere in particular?" Chloe called, looking around at the empty seats of the auditorium.

"Nope, you pick!" said Hanna, laughing.

And then, Eva started the music, and the show began.

The four KIDZ BOP Kids were lined up on the stage ready to run through their entire concert to show Chloe that they could still perform, even without Elijah. Hanna had a whole swarm of butterflies in her stomach. She could see Chloe sitting out in the auditorium. This had to be the performance of a lifetime.

Elijah had several dance solos in the show, and now there was no one to do them. "What do we do in those spots?" Eva had asked, as they began to discuss their plan.

"Easy!" Steffan had said, remembering Charisma dancing to Elijah's "Just a Dream" solo earlier in the day. "We improvise!"

So, when Elijah's first solo arrived, Charisma performed it with her own special flair. Not only did she perform the choreography to perfection, she added some cheerleading gymnastics as a special touch. During Elijah's second solo, Eva threw in some moves that hinted at her ballet roots. When their turns came, Hanna worked in some modern dance, and Steffan did some freestyle of his own.

"Woo hoo!" the kids heard Chloe shout from her seat.

The four KIDZ BOP Kids looked around at each other. They all wore matching grins of absolute triumph. This was going to work!

When "Naturally" started, Hanna felt a tiny nudge and turned to see Eva looking at her. "You do it this time," Eva mouthed and smiled.

And so Hanna performed the solo that she and Eva had both wanted so much. Although she had sung the solo a million times on her own, she felt nervous as the words poured out of her mouth. She felt happy knowing that Eva would be singing it in the concert. When it was over, Chloe shouted, *"Yes, Hanna!"* from her seat and clapped loudly. Hanna did not stop grinning for the rest of the performance.

"Well, are you convinced?" asked Charisma. She, Eva, Steffan, and Hanna stood in the middle of the stage where they had just run through the entire show flawlessly. Even without Elijah, it was a powerhouse performance.

"Oh, I'm convinced . . . that you're all nuts," said Chloe. "But I'm willing to give your plan a chance. If you guys want to use the promotional tour to find someone to replace Elijah, then, as your manager, I will do everything I can to help you out. Besides, this contest would be good exposure for the group."

"Woo hoo!" shouted Hanna.

"Well, we need to get planning!" said Charisma, giddily rubbing her hands together. "We leave in just a few days!"

Three days later, at 6 A.M., Eva, Steffan, Charisma, and Hanna were standing on the curb with their suitcases lined up next to them. They were waiting for Chloe to arrive. She had gone to pick up the rental van that they would be taking on the tour.

"You guys will love the tour van," said Chloe. "I just hope we have enough room for all of Eva's hats and Steffan's guitar."

The flurry of packing had resulted in a lot of luggage.

"I wonder how many hats I can fit into my suitcase and still be able to bring all the clothes I need," said Eva, pondering her hat collection.

"Hats!?" Charisma exclaimed. "What about shoes? I'm going to need so many shoes for this trip."

But the kids were way too excited to worry about being crowded. They were going out on their promotional tour!

Thanks to Chloe, bright and early the morning after their surprise concert, the KIDZ BOP website had a huge banner posted on it with the words "Be a KIDZ BOP Kid for a day!" The dates and locations of auditions were listed below. Any kid who wanted to join the KIDZ BOP Kids could try out and join them for a special performance in New York. It was a dream come true for anyone who saw it. They would have hundreds, if not thousands, of kids auditioning in every city. Chloe had stayed up most of the last three nights scheduling theaters for the auditions to take place.

But she didn't look the least bit tired when she arrived a few minutes later. She looked downright giddy. Rather than arriving in a rental van, Chloe had arrived in a long, sleek tour bus. The words "KIDZ BOP Kids" had been painted on the sides in bright blue writing. The doors opened, and Chloe came down the steps with a grin on her face.

"I thought we were waiting on a van," said Charisma. "This? Is not a van."

"Silly me," Chloe said. "Did I say 'van'? I meant 'your own personal tour bus.'"

"Chicago, here we come," said Steffan.

Chapter 12
The Windy City Auditions

It was not hard to figure out where the KIDZ BOP auditions were taking place in Chicago. There was a line of kids around the block in front of one of the big downtown theaters. And when the KIDZ BOP Kids' tour bus pulled up to the front of the theater, all of them began to cheer.

"There must be a thousand people here," said Eva, looking out the window.

"I certainly didn't expect this," said Chloe. "I'll have the driver pull right up to the door. Just go right in."

"I feel like a total celeb right now!" said Charisma. "No time to even sign autographs."

The other kids laughed. For the first time, they really did feel famous. Now, all they needed was a red carpet!

When the KIDZ BOP Kids stepped down from the bus, the crowd roared. The auditioners closest to them began to snap the Kids' pictures on their camera phones. The KIDZ BOP Kids knew that their audition videos and bios had been posted online, but they had no idea that this many people even knew who they were yet. It was very exciting!

"Sorry, we're in a rush to get inside," Chloe called to the crowd. But be sure to stick around for the autograph signing afterward!"

As part of the promotional tour, every day after auditions, the KIDZ BOP Kids would have a meet and greet with fans, sign autographs, and pose for some pictures.

"Welcome to Chicago!" A short blond woman with glasses approached the KIDZ BOP Kids when they got inside the theater.

"Thank you!" said Hanna, shaking her hand.

"I'm Addy," the woman said. "The record company hired me to run the auditions here. Are you ready?"

"Yep!" said Charisma enthusiastically. The crowd outside got her very excited for auditions. The newest KIDZ BOP Kid might be right outside!

"Here's what will happen," said Addy. "We're screening the auditioners in another room. The ones we like, we'll send in to you for a second audition. And then you guys get to pick a finalist. Sound like a plan?"

The KIDZ BOP Kids nodded.

"Then, grab a seat in the auditorium, and we'll get started."

It turned out that watching other people audition was not as exciting as the KIDZ BOP Kids expected. Four hours into auditions with only a short break for lunch, the kids were already worn out.

The first person to audition was a piano virtuoso with a killer voice. Her song was amazing, but her dancing was only subpar. The second person to audition had amazing dance moves, but when he opened his mouth to sing, the KIDZ BOP Kids all cringed. Every potential KIDZ BOP Kid who stepped up to audition was not quite right.

As they watched, the kids couldn't help remembering their own audition experiences. Each KIDZ BOP Kid had sent in a carefully made audition tape—after many failed attempts at a good performance. Steffan had set up his tripod and then promptly kicked it over when he did a back flip for the camera. Hanna's younger brother had walked in as the camcorder recorded and started singing along with her. Eva broke three guitar strings as she rocked her way through the Ting Tings' "That's Not My Name." And

Charisma's first attempt at an audition tape involved her falli. into the crack between the bed and the wall in her bedroom and getting stuck. So, for every auditioner who came onstage and sang and danced his or her heart out, each of the KIDZ BOP Kids had a feeling of disappointment on their behalf. No one was quite right, but they didn't want to disappoint anyone!

"We'll watch one more audition, and then we'll head out to the main entrance for the signing," said Chloe.

The final person to audition walked out onto the stage. He carried a guitar.

"I'm Ben," he said, waving to the KIDZ BOP Kids. And then he began to play. As the song continued, Steffan's eyes grew larger and larger. Out of all of them, he could appreciate a skilled guitar player the most. And Ben was playing one of his favorite Coldplay songs. Immediately, Steffan began to imagine the KIDZ BOP Kids with Ben as part of the group. It would be completely awesome! They could jam together.

When the audition was over and Ben left the stage, Eva said, "Well?"

"He was *awesome*!" said Steffan. "I think we've found our new KIDZ BOP Kid!"

Hanna raised an eyebrow and frowned. "I don't know," she said.

"What? He was great!" said Steffan.

"I agree with you, but I still don't think he's quite right," Hanna replied quietly.

"She's right," said Eva. "I didn't think his dance performance was all that."

"But he had some pretty great style," said Charisma. She had liked Ben as much as Steffan did, and she was disappointed that they didn't all agree.

"Maybe you just don't like him because he's not Elijah," Steffan suggested.

"Remember, we still have four other cities to visit," said Chloe. "Shall we make Ben your Chicago finalist?"

Begrudgingly, the KIDZ BOP Kids agreed.

Hanna nibbled a cookie from the suite's mini fridge when they got back to the hotel. The ride from the theater had been a fairly silent one. Everyone was still thinking about the final audition and how easily the group fell apart over a minor disagreement. After all the effort they had made to work together as a team, could it still all fall down around them without Elijah holding the group together?

Hanna settled down in a big chair with *New Moon*, and tried to wipe away the worry from her day.

Soon, Steffan joined her, sitting in a chair nearby with the copy of *Twilight* she'd loaned him. He smiled and held up the book for her to see. Then, he opened it and began to read.

Tomorrow morning, they would be doing an interview with a popular music blogger. Then, they would be making an appearance on a local radio program to discuss the concert they would be doing in Chicago in the next few months. Then, they would be leaving for Cleveland where they would see more auditions. By the end of the week, they will have made their way down to Florida. And then, back to New York to continue to rehearse like mad. But for that moment, Hanna and Steffan read and ate cookies on the balcony of their hotel suite, overlooking downtown Chicago and Lake Michigan stretching out beyond it into the distance.

Chapter 13
Hot in Cleveland and Miami

The drive from Chicago to Cleveland would take about six hours, so the KIDZ BOP Kids had a lot of time to hang out on the bus and just enjoy the ride.

"Fashion show time!" Eva said, clapping her hands. "You'll never guess what I got for all of you!"

As the KIDZ BOP Kids watched, Eva opened her suitcase and brought out five Chicago Cubs caps.

"I buy a hat in every city I visit," Eva explained. "This time I got hats for all of you! Now, we'll never forget the time we drove around the country looking for a new KIDZ BOP Kid!"

"Who's the fifth hat for?" Steffan asked.

Eva smiled. "Elijah, of course."

Elijah hadn't exactly been overjoyed when the KIDZ BOP Kids broke the news to him that they would need to find someone new to join them onstage for the New York concert. But after they explained that when he recovered Elijah would take back his old place with the group, he felt much happier. Still, they couldn't help but feel bad about replacing their friend. The New York concert meant a lot to him. And it was their first performance as a group!

The KIDZ BOP Kids took turns trying on the hats that Eva had gotten for them and walking down the aisle in the bus like it was their private catwalk.

When the tour bus finally rolled into Cleveland, the KIDZ BOP Kids made their way up to their hotel suite for a quick change of clothing before heading to the next set of auditions.

None of the KIDZ BOP Kids had visited Cleveland before, so as they drove through the city, they looked out the windows of the bus.

"There's the Terminal Tower," said Hanna, pointing. She had a Cleveland visitor's guide that she had gotten at the hotel open in her lap. Checking out the famous landmarks had always been Hanna's favorite part of family vacations. She had to keep the tradition alive!

The crowd in Cleveland was even bigger than the crowd in Chicago. Word was getting around, and more and more kids wanted to try their luck at auditioning to be a KIDZ BOP Kid.

At the end of the second day of auditions, the Kids had chosen a second finalist, Sara, the lead singer of a local band. Eva smiled approvingly at Sara's pink dyed hair and striped knee-high socks. She loved a gal with style, and Sara had plenty of that—not to mention a killer voice and amazing dance moves.

Steffan was still thinking about Ben back in Chicago, Charisma was now torn between the two finalists, and Hanna still hadn't seen anyone she completely approved of. But the KIDZ BOP Kids tried their best to keep their opinions to themselves as much as possible. No one wanted another huge argument.

As the KIDZ BOP Kids signed autographs for excited fans, all of them couldn't help but be preoccupied with the task at hand. Eva was so distracted with her own thoughts that she accidentally signed, "To Tiffanie, Love Eva," for a fan. After the fan responded, "Hey! My name is Stephanie!" Eva sat in her chair timid and red-faced until the signing was over.

"Well, we need to head back to the hotel," Chloe said. "You guys have a television interview in an hour, and we have to get you camera ready!"

A morning two days later found the KIDZ BOP Kids and their manager on the long drive to Miami, Florida. Luckily, Miami was the last stop on the tour, and then they could head back to New York. But the drive was the longest of their trip, and none of them were looking forward to it.

"I have an idea," said Charisma. "Why don't I teach you guys a cheer? That's what we do on the long drives to cheer competitions. It makes things go much faster."

The KIDZ BOP Kids all agreed, and soon time on the bus was melting away as they launched into a few of Charisma's favorite cheers, followed by catnaps all around. The tour had worn everyone out.

When the KIDZ BOP Kids arrived in Miami to the humid air and palm trees, they saw that the crowd lined up for auditions was the biggest yet. There was a security team blocking the doors to keep people from going inside. They only stepped aside to let the KIDZ BOP Kids pass.

It turned out that Florida was filled with terrific performers, and at the end of the day, the KIDZ BOP Kids had a terrible time deciding on a finalist. They spent most of the evening talking about each performer. As they sat down to a meal of warm pizza out by the pool at their hotel, they finally agreed on Cruz. The Miami native was full of energy and danced in a way that rivaled even Elijah's skill.

"If we had to choose right now, I would pick Cruz out of all the finalists," Hanna announced.

"Let's take a vote in the morning when we're all rested," Chloe said.

"Can I ask you something, Chloe?" Charisma asked, from where she was sitting with her feet dangling into the pool.

"Sure," Chloe replied.

"How did you get Madison Day to agree to let us open for her anyway? We've all been wondering."

Chloe laughed. "Oh, Tay and I go way back! I choreographed her very first Grammy appearance," she said proudly. "She danced so well, after the Grammys were over she told me that if I ever needed a favor, to give her a call. Anything! So a couple of months ago, I called her up and told her I had a great idea for an opening act for her New York show. And she agreed."

"Wow, that's so cool," said Charisma. She had a faraway look in her eyes, imagining being able to call Madison Day up out of the blue.

"Oh, and I talked to her last night, and she can't wait to meet you guys!" said Chloe. If Charisma had been sitting in a chair, she would have fallen out of it in excitement.

The day had come. The KIDZ BOP Kids had to decide who would replace Elijah. The drive back to New York would take hours, and it was during that time the KIDZ BOP Kids would sit and talk about their final decision. On the tiny table where the KIDZ BOP Kids had their meals while traveling on the bus, Chloe laid out three pieces of paper. One paper had "Ben" written on it. One said "Sara," and the third had "Cruz" written in bold marker.

"Eva," said Chloe, "Why don't you take notes?"

Eva went to her suitcase and got out her notebook and pen and sat back down at the table with her friends.

"I think we can all agree that all of the finalists you've selected are amazing and talented people, and any one of them would be an excellent KIDZ BOP Kid. So, really, the question is which of these finalists would be able to fit in and learn the choreography the fastest? Remember, it's not about your favorites. It's about what's best for the group. So, keep that in mind."

The KIDZ BOP Kids all nodded.

"Steffan, which finalist do you think would be the best choice to join our group?" Chloe asked.

"Easy," said Steffan. "Ben."

"Why?" Chloe asked.

And as Eva furiously scribbled down what he said in her notepad, Steffan outlined exactly why he thought Ben would be an amazing KIDZ BOP Kid, from his friendly attitude at the audition to his skill as a musician.

"But can he pick up the choreography fast enough?" Hanna asked the whole group.

"Of course he can!" said Steffan.

"How do you know?" said Hanna.

"Because I saw him dance!" Steffan said, almost angrily. No one had ever really seen Steffan get upset or angry about anything.

"I don't know," Hanna said. "I think we want a stronger dancer and should go with Cruz. When it came to dancing, Ben was good, but Cruz was better."

"What about Sara?" asked Eva. "Sara was a strong dancer. And her vocal audition was awesome."

"I'm not disagreeing," said Hanna, carefully. "But I still think Cruz is our best option."

"What do you think, Charisma?" Chloe asked. Up until that point, Charisma had remained sitting in her seat staring down at the table, deep in thought.

Charisma had been dreading this moment. She didn't know how to answer. She had liked all of the finalists, and making a decision like this brought her back to their last cheerleader tryout when she had been left to pick the new member of the squad. She hated to disappoint anyone.

"I . . . I don't know," said Charisma at last, shaking her head. "I think they're all good." She shrugged.

The other KIDZ BOP Kids opened their mouths to protest, but Chloe held up her hand to quiet them.

"Well, there's not a fair way to make a vote here," she said. "So, what do we do?"

"Maybe there's a way to determine once and for all, without voting, who the best finalist is without putting it to a vote," said Eva.

"Hey!" said Steffan. "I have an idea."

Chapter 14
The KIDZ BOP Music Video Runoff!

Everyone leaned in to hear Steffan's plan.

"We can give them a test," said Steffan. "Something to help us decide. Whoever wins is our final choice."

The other three KIDZ BOP Kids looked skeptical.

"We ask them for a final audition. They have to go to a famous landmark in their city and put on an impromptu concert. Today even—to see how resourceful they can be. Whoever puts on the best show with the best turnout wins and gets to perform with us in New York," Steffan explained.

"How do we know how the concert goes?" asked Eva. "We'll be in New York."

"Easy. They have someone film it," said Steffan. "Then, they send us their videos."

"That might work," said Chloe. "What do the rest of you think?"

"I'm for it," said Charisma.

Eva and Hanna both nodded as well.

"Do you think this will work?" Eva whispered so that only Hanna could hear her.

"It has to," Hanna replied. "We don't have time to look for anybody else."

★

The KIDZ BOP Kids were happy to see the bright lights of New York again. Eva gazed out happily at her city from the window of the bus and sighed. She had never been so excited to see Manhattan. Home at last!

Typical for New York in the summer, the air was hot and humid as the KIDZ BOP Kids left the air-conditioned comfort of the bus and walked up the steps of their hotel.

"Well, we have a video from Sara," said Chloe, glancing down at her BlackBerry.

"Oh! I can't wait to watch it," said Eva with excitement.

"I'll download it when we get upstairs," said Chloe. "We can even watch it in HD."

The KIDZ BOP suite was just like they had left it. Eva's extra hats and Charisma's shoes were just where they had left them, and there were piles of sheet music on the tables.

"Home suite home," said Hanna. "Get it? Suite?"

"Waaaa waaaaaah," said Steffan.

"Oh, come on. It was funny," said Hanna, punching him in the arm with a grin. Steffan seemed to have forgiven her for disagreeing about who should be the new KIDZ BOP Kid. Hanna was glad.

Sara's concert video was filmed in Public Square in downtown Cleveland, right next to the statue of General Moses Cleaveland, the founder of the Ohio city. There were hundreds of people milling about.

"Hey, KIDZ BOP Kids. This concert is brought to you by Sara Collins, future KIDZ BOP Kid, and the gods of rock," Sara said into the camera, pink hair gleaming in the afternoon sunlight.

As Sara and her band began to play, the KIDZ BOP Kids saw more and more people gathering around to listen. There were some people cheering the band on, and others who just looked confused. But the best part was the people in the crowd who began to clap along and cheer and clamor to get a glimpse of the band. Sara knew how to a pick a venue, that was for sure.

Sara sang and danced to the music, moving with the kind of original style that had been the reason the KIDZ BOP Kids had picked her as a finalist in the first place. There was no question. She was completely talented and would be an amazing addition to their group.

At the end of the concert, Sara and her band took a bow, and Sara herself waved into the camera.

"See you soon, KIDZ BOP Kids!" she said. And then the camera was shut off, and the Kids were left staring at snow on the television screen.

"Well . . ." said Steffan. "Eva's right. She does have style."

Ben's video arrived next in Chloe's inbox. He had taken a slightly different approach to the impromptu concert, grabbing his guitar and heading up to the observation deck of the Sears Tower, the tallest building in North America and a popular Chicago landmark.

"My dad is one of the security guards up here," Ben said, grinning into the camera. "This is my concert, from the one-hundred-third story of the Sears Tower. I hope you enjoy it!" With that, he began to play a few of his favorite songs. Then, to show off his dance moves, he put on some music and did some freestyle. All the while, visitors to the Sears Tower gathered around to watch the show. Some people even threw money. One man even introduced himself as a record producer and gave Ben his card.

"I hate to say this," said Charisma. "But it's still a toss-up for me. Sara and Ben both put on really awesome concerts."

"Well, let's wait and see how we all feel after we watch Cruz's video," Chloe said.

The KIDZ BOP Kids were slightly worried when Cruz's concert video hadn't shown up by seven o'clock that evening.

"I tried calling his cell phone," said Chloe. "I left him a message saying that if we didn't get his video by eight, we would have to disqualify him."

As the minutes slowly ticked by, and no one heard from their Miami finalist, the KIDZ BOP Kids began to realize that they might only get the two finalists to choose from. Maybe Cruz couldn't make a video on time. Or perhaps, he had just lost interest in being a KIDZ BOP Kid.

At 7:59 P.M., his video finally arrived.

"Sorry this is so late," his e-mail read. "But I was waiting for the 6:00 news to come on. Enjoy!"

Chloe downloaded the video and pushed play. The KIDZ BOP Kids gathered around to watch. The video started with Cruz standing in the center of Sun Life Stadium, home of the Florida Marlins, Miami's professional baseball team. He had his hand over his heart, and he was singing the national anthem. As the footage rolled, a TV reporter began to speak.

"For one lucky baseball fan, tonight was a dream come true when Florida Marlins starting pitcher Josh Johnson spotted him performing outside of the stadium and was so impressed, he invited him into the clubhouse to meet the team. Cruz Velasquez of Miami was even invited by the team's owners to perform the national anthem before the game."

"We just thought he was a talented guy," said Josh Johnson into the camera. "A kid like that deserves a shot at fame, and I was happy to help out."

There, the news footage ended, and the video showed Cruz singing and dancing for the Florida Marlins in the locker room after the game. The players were all laughing and clapping along to the beat. The concert ended with high-fives all around. One player even said, "Cruz, you're our good luck charm. We wouldn't have won today without you."

And then Cruz looked into the camera and said, "See you soon, KIDZ BOP Kids!"

The KIDZ BOP Kids looked around at each other, mouths agape.

"Well, that was certainly the biggest crowd of all the finalists," said Hanna.

"Welcome to the KIDZ BOP Kids, Cruz," Eva said aloud. Nods all around showed that everyone was finally in agreement.

Chapter 15
A Cruz-in' Good Luck Charm!

"**W**elcome to New York, Cruz Velasquez," muttered Cruz to himself as he walked through the doors at LaGuardia Airport and looked around. So, this was New York? This was Cruz's first visit. The farthest he had traveled from home before now was a drive to Orlando to visit Disney World. And now he was in the Big Apple!

When Chloe, the KIDZ BOP Kids' manager, had called him the night before and told him how much they loved his video and wanted him in New York ASAP to begin rehearsing with the group, he could barely contain his excitement. Just yesterday, through some crazy luck, he'd met the Florida Marlins! Things were going good for Cruz. He hoped the luck kept coming. He needed it, especially with his mom losing her job a few weeks before. They'd barely made it to the airport in their old broken-down car.

"Good luck, *mi hijo!*" his mom had said, kissing his cheek. He could almost still smell her perfume now, standing outside the doors of the airport hundreds of miles away.

"Mr. Velasquez?" said a voice nearby. Cruz looked up to see a limo driver carrying a sign with his name written on it. Well, this was going to be a new experience.

★

Eva was hard at work most of the morning, overseeing the decoration of the suite for Cruz's arrival.

"I want him to feel welcome!" she said, handing a string of lights to Charisma and Hanna.

Meanwhile, Steffan was putting up a sign that said "Welcome, Cruz!" on the door.

Eva herself was in the tiny suite kitchen putting some brownies on a plate and pouring cups of juice for everyone.

While the suite didn't look as good as it had on the day the KIDZ BOP Kids all first arrived, given that they only had a few hours to decorate, it still looked pretty amazing as Eva and the other KIDZ BOP Kids stepped back to admire their handiwork.

"Cruz is arriving early!" Chloe exclaimed, bursting out of her room in the suite, her cell phone clutched in her hand. "Oh!" she said, looking around. "I see you're already prepared. Well, Cruz's car just left the airport. And we have to get to rehearsal pretty much right after he gets here." Chloe looked at her watch impatiently. After working with Chloe for the time that they had, the KIDZ BOP Kids knew that nothing annoyed her more than being off schedule.

"We'll get ready to go," Hanna reassured her.

"What on earth did I do with my glasses?" Chloe asked, looking around and patting her pockets to check for them. The KIDZ BOP Kids stepped aside as she rushed over to the sofa and began to lift the cushions to look for her missing glasses.

"Oh!" Chloe said and pulled something from beneath one of the cushions. "Looks like Elijah left this behind."

It was Elijah's whoopee cushion. And despite the cheerful decorations welcoming Cruz to New York all around them, the

KIDZ BOP Kids all suddenly had an overwhelming feeling of sadness as they silently missed their friend.

When Cruz entered the hotel lobby and looked up at the high, chandeliered ceilings and saw bellhops in crisp uniforms, he realized he had never felt so out of place in his life. This was like a movie, and he was the unlikely star.

As Cruz approached the front desk, the woman behind the counter immediately handed him a key and said, "Take this key and head right up to the top floor, Mr. Velasquez."

"Let me get that for you," said one of the bellhops, and took his bag. Cruz felt strange walking toward the elevators with nothing in his hand but a small plastic rectangle that looked nothing like a key.

He felt even stranger when he stepped from the elevator and saw the door to the KIDZ BOP suite. It was covered with balloons and streamers, like they were in the middle of a parade route. Was this all for him?

Suddenly, the door burst open, and a girl with light brown hair popped her head out and said, "He's here, everybody! Welcome, Cruz! I'm Charisma." She grabbed him into a hug and then stepped aside to let him enter the room.

Eva stepped up to shake his hand next and offer him a brownie, followed by Hanna and then Steffan.

Cruz had seen all the KIDZ BOP Kids before at the audition, but this was the first time he'd met them face to face. They were all nice enough, but Cruz thought they all seemed a bit glum or something. And despite being a generally friendly, fun-loving guy who was usually the life of the party, for the first time, Cruz felt slightly awkward and out of place.

The KIDZ BOP Kids, their manager, and their newest member hopped on the subway heading downtown.

"What do you think of New York so far?" Charisma asked Cruz, who was sitting next to her on the subway looking around curiously.

"Well, I've only seen the hotel room and now the subway," said Cruz, with a smile, "But I guess I like it." He was still thinking about the strange feeling he had back in the hotel suite, like he had interrupted something. But Charisma seemed nice enough. Cruz had heard she was a cheerleader back home, and she certainly was cheerful.

"We'll take you on a tour of the city sometime," Charisma reassured him. "Is there anyplace you would like to visit?"

Cruz thought about it for a second.

"How about Coney Island?" he said. If Cruz could at least see the ocean, it might feel a little more like Miami. Two hours in New York, and he was feeling slightly homesick.

"I'll talk to Chloe about it," said Charisma with a smile. "I haven't been there either, and I want to go on the roller coaster! Eva keeps talking about it."

"But first, I have to get through my first day of rehearsal," Cruz muttered under his breath.

Chapter 16
The Water Balloon Cure

Elijah was sleeping with his sore ankle propped up on a pillow when his mom opened his bedroom door and peeked in.

"Elijah!" she said, trying to rouse him.

"I'm sleeping, Mom," he replied, pulling his other pillow from his face, where he had placed it to block out the light.

"Are you gonna spend the whole day in bed? It's almost 11:30," Elijah's mom asked.

"Nah, I was going to get up and have a bowl of cereal soon and then watch some TV. Then, go back to bed."

Elijah's mom rolled her eyes. "I know you're disappointed about the concert, Elijah," she said. "If Dr. Miller gives the okay, you can go back to New York in a few weeks. I promise."

"It won't be the same. The concert will be over by then," Elijah replied.

Elijah had another appointment with the family doctor that afternoon for a second round of X-rays. Since arriving home from New York, he had been doing nothing but playing Xbox and watching TV.

"Have you heard from anyone in the group?" Elijah's mom asked.

"Steffan e-mailed me yesterday, and Hanna sent me a virtual toilet seat."

"They know you too well."

"I guess."

"Why don't you call them?" said Elijah's mom.

Elijah sighed. "They're probably in rehearsal."

"I'm sure they won't mind."

"They have to rehearse. The show is in just a few weeks. I don't want to interrupt."

"They'll be happy to hear from you no matter what. Just call them. I'm tired of you moping around." Elijah's mom got up, handed her son his cell phone, and left the room.

All of the KIDZ BOP Kids had cell phones with each other's phone numbers plugged in just in case there was an emergency. Elijah had been turning his phone on all morning and clicking through their numbers one by one and then setting the phone down again. Finally, he scrolled down to Steffan's cell phone number and pushed "dial."

Steffan answered almost immediately. "Elijah!" he said.

"Yeah, man. It's me. What's going on there? Are you guys having a party? I can barely hear you," said Elijah.

"Chloe's got the sound system way up to prepare us for Madison Square Garden," said Steffan.

"That's awesome," said Elijah.

"How's your ankle?" Steffan asked.

"It's okay," Elijah replied. "I'm going in for more X-rays in a while."

"I hope they turn out all right," said Steffan.

"Me too."

"Hopefully we'll be seeing you again soon," said Steffan. "We miss you."

"Yeah," said Elijah.

"So, I don't know if Chloe talked to you yet today, but we found someone to replace you for the Madison Square Garden concert," said Steffan, a hint of wariness in his voice.

Elijah sighed. "Yeah, she called me. It's okay," he said. "You guys couldn't exactly go on without me, right? Did you at least find somebody good?"

"Yeah," said Steffan. "This guy, Cruz, from Miami. He's a pretty good dancer."

"Well, that's good," said Elijah.

"Listen, I gotta go, bro," said Steffan. "I'll call you back tonight?"

"Sounds good," said Elijah.

"All right, man," said Steffan. "Talk to you soon."

"Tell Cruz I said congratulations," said Elijah. But Steffan had already hung up. There was silence on the other end.

When Elijah had gotten the call to join the KIDZ BOP Kids, it was the happiest moment of his entire life. For the first time, he felt like he fit in somewhere. When he danced, people took notice. They didn't roll their eyes and say, "Teacher! Elijah is dancing again." They cheered him on. But when he hurt his ankle, Elijah began to feel all of that slipping away. Being a KIDZ BOP Kid was his life. And now all he could do was go to doctor's appointments and not put any weight on his ankle until it healed. It was pretty lame. And boring!

"Well, did you talk to them?" Elijah's mom was back, popping her head in his doorway.

"Yeah, they found a new group member," Elijah replied.

"That's good!" said his mom.

"I guess," said Elijah. "They all sounded pretty happy." He shrugged.

"Well, I know what would make *you* happy," said Elijah's mom.

Elijah felt doubtful. His two favorite things were dancing and basketball. Neither of which he could do on a sore ankle. "What's that?" he asked.

"Helping me ambush your dad with the water balloon launcher when he gets home." Elijah's mom's eyes twinkled with mischief.

"Do we have enough balloons?" Elijah asked.

Elijah felt slightly better as he filled water balloons with the garden hose and crouched in wait for his father to pull into the driveway. But the idea of Cruz taking his place was still on Elijah's mind. What if, when this was all over, the other kids decided that Cruz was a better performer? What if they decided to replace Elijah permanently?

Elijah tried to imagine the KIDZ BOP Kids onstage performing at Madison Square Garden without him. He wanted his friends to go forward with the show. They had all worked so hard. Why should one ankle injury stop the rest of them? But now Elijah wasn't so sure it was the best idea. The fans would be shouting, "Cruz! Cruz! Cruz!" But what about Elijah? He had worked so hard. Would he still be a part of the group when his ankle healed?

He had an appointment to get another X-ray tomorrow. The doctor said there was a small chance the injury would heal on its own. What if . . . just what if it could be healed just in time for the KIDZ BOP concert? Would Elijah be able to dance?

Elijah wasn't sure what to do, but he knew he had to do something. And soon.

Chapter 17
Singin' the KIDZ BOP Blues

Steffan felt terrible. First, they'd found Elijah's whoopee cushion right before Cruz arrived. And then, in the middle of their first rehearsal with him, Elijah called. Steffan already felt guilty about replacing his friend. But hearing the disappointment in Elijah's voice had been too much. Had they been selfish to allow the show to go on without one of its stars? Steffan had begun to wonder.

Steffan watched as Chloe demonstrated a piece of the choreography for Cruz and then watched approvingly as he picked it up. His dance skills were on a par with Elijah's. But he wasn't Elijah. And maybe that was harder for Steffan to deal with than he had originally thought.

"Was that Elijah on the phone earlier?" Hanna said, sitting down next to Steffan.

"Yeah," Steffan replied.

"Did you tell him I said 'hi'?" asked Hanna, elbowing him in the ribs.

Steffan chuckled. "No, I didn't."

"He knows about Cruz," Steffan continued with a shrug. "He seems fine, but I can't shake that guilty feeling."

"I'm feeling it too," said Hanna with a nod. "I wish I knew what to do about it."

"Okay, everyone up here to work through the choreography for 'Club Can't Handle Me'!" Chloe called.

The KIDZ BOP Kids lined up and began to run through the song. To make things easier this late in the game, Cruz would just do all of Elijah's vocal and dance solos. Of course, he could add his own special flair for the Latino beat. The other KIDZ BOP Kids watched in awe as he picked up the choreography immediately and shined when it came time for him to do his first solo. Everything seemed to be going well. Unfortunately, that didn't last too long.

Cruz sat down on the edge of the stage, his feet dangling out into the auditorium, and took a sip of his water. He had never danced so hard in his life. Chloe was a great teacher, but Cruz was already sore from learning the choreography and keeping up with the others.

He looked around at the other KIDZ BOP Kids from where he was sitting. They were all great dancers, and the rest of them seemed to know the routine pretty well. Cruz just hoped he could keep up, and that soon he would start feeling like a part of the group. No one had really spoken to him since rehearsal began that day. Even Charisma, who had chatted with him on the subway, was across the stage talking to Chloe. Cruz supposed it was up to him to make friends. So, he stood up and went over to where Hanna was sitting.

"Hey," said Cruz.

"Hey," Hanna replied, smiling.

"Is rehearsal always this crazy?" Cruz said.

Hanna chuckled. "You'll go to bed sore every day for a while, but you'll get used to it,"

"I just hope I can pick up the choreography in time for the show. I'm so far behind," said Cruz.

"Well, if you need extra help, I know Chloe would be happy to help you," Hanna replied.

"I'll have to ask her," Cruz said, getting that awkward feeling again, like he'd just interrupted Hanna in the middle of something.

Just then Eva arrived at Hanna's side, carrying two bottles of water.

"Oh!" Eva said, looking at Cruz and back down at the bottles of water in her hand. "I only brought two, but there's more over there." She pointed. Cruz knew when he wasn't wanted. He'd walked over with water already in his hand. Why would Eva say that to him unless she wanted him to go away?

Cruz looked around at the other KIDZ BOP Kids. Steffan was staring down at the cell phone in his hand. Charisma was leaning against the piano talking to Chloe. And Cruz suddenly felt lonely standing there. He walked back over to the edge of the stage and sat back down again.

The rest of rehearsal was an utter disaster. Eva broke a lace in her dance shoe. Hanna missed two different cues and missed one of her solos entirely. Steffan was apparently in another world for most of the rehearsal, and Charisma kicked over a speaker.

"No, Hanna," Chloe called. "Left foot! Left foot!"

"Sorry, Chloe!" said Hanna and hurried to catch up. Everyone seemed to suddenly have two left feet. Granted, it had been a week since they had really rehearsed together, but this went beyond falling out of practice. Things were just . . . different, almost somber somehow.

Chloe looked at her group. Cruz was working through the routine in a skilled, but unenthusiastic, way. Steffan hadn't really said much to anyone since the beginning of rehearsal. Eva's dancing was a disaster. Hanna was missing her cues. Even Charisma seemed to be struggling to hold on to a positive attitude. Chloe knew that they were missing Elijah. Whether she wanted to admit it or not, Elijah had been the group's unofficial leader, motivating them and making them laugh.

These were not the same enthusiastic KIDZ BOP Kids who had convinced her to let them continue rehearsing for the Madison Day show. Something was definitely not right—and that needed to change if they were going to perform in front of thousands of fans in just a few weeks.

That night, the other KIDZ BOP Kids gathered in the living room to play some video games in an attempt to cheer themselves up.

"Hey, Cruz! *KIDZ BOP Dance Party!*" said Charisma, knocking on his door. "And we're ordering pizza pretty soon!" None of them had really talked to Cruz since they'd gotten back from rehearsal.

But Cruz wasn't in the mood to socialize.

"I think I'm going to read a book," he said with a shrug. Charisma nodded and left. She hoped that it wasn't anything she had done to offend him.

But after that day of rehearsal, Cruz was positive that, apart from Charisma who was pretty much a friend to all, the other KIDZ BOP Kids didn't like him. Rehearsals were going badly, and somehow he felt like it was his fault or something. Cruz couldn't help but wonder, was that a look of disappointment on Eva's face when he messed up on the choreography? Was Steffan's quietness part of his personality, or did he resent Cruz being here instead of his friend? Cruz couldn't tell for sure, but he didn't like it.

PART 3

Chapter 18
Odd Man Out

"**G**rab your stuff, KIDZ BOP Kids!" said Chloe, her voice brimming with excitement. "Today, we go to the theater!"

Chloe was trying hard to help the KIDZ BOP Kids and their new group member get along. And the tension had grown high since their disastrous first rehearsal. So, today they were taking time out of rehearsal to see a Broadway performance of *The Lion King*—and hopefully forge some kind of bond with their new member.

Dressed to the nines, the gang headed outside into Times Square and made their way toward the theater. Times Square was bustling with tourists carrying shopping bags and cameras. In a few weeks, maybe a few of these people would be lined up outside of Madison Square Garden waiting for the KIDZ BOP Kids' show to start.

"*The Lion King*. Omigosh!" Hanna said with excitement. This was her first real Broadway show. She'd seen the movie a million times, but this was totally different. There would be costumes and dancing!

"You'll have to save your very first Playbill as a keepsake," said Eva, looping her arm through Hanna's as they strolled along. She had a whole book of Playbills at home and fond memories of all of the Broadway shows she had seen. It was exciting to accompany her friends to their first Broadway performance!

When they got to the theater, the KIDZ BOP Kids took their seats, and to his dismay Cruz found himself sitting next to Steffan. "Oh, great," he thought, seeing Steffan's half-hearted smile in his direction when he saw where he was sitting.

"Have you ever been to a Broadway show?" Cruz asked Steffan, trying to be friendly.

"No, you?" Steffan replied.

"No," said Cruz. He started to ask another question and figured he would probably get the same short response. "I give up," he thought to himself. "No sense in jumping through hoops to make friends who don't seem interested."

Cruz leaned his head on his hand and prepared to watch the show.

Two and a half hours later, the KIDZ BOP Kids burst from the theater into the bright New York afternoon.

"Well, what did you think?" Chloe asked.

"*Amazing!*" said Hanna, hugging her Playbill to her chest.

"I loved it," said Charisma, dreamily.

"Good," said Chloe. "I hope you took notes because there's going to be a pop quiz when we get to rehearsal."

The KIDZ BOP Kids all groaned. Back at the rehearsal theater, Chloe made them all sit in a circle on the stage.

"Tell me," she said, passing around some granola bars, "What is keeping us from being as good as the dancers on that stage today?"

"Is this a pop quiz?" Eva asked. "I thought you were going to ask us who played Mustafa and stuff like that."

Chloe laughed. "No, this is different."

The KIDZ BOP Kids looked around at each other. They were all talented singers and dancers. And yet the performances they had seen that afternoon were ten times better than the way they were currently rehearsing.

"What does this have to do with us?" Steffan asked.

"Everything," said Chloe.

"She wants us to say 'teamwork,' you guys," said Cruz, a bored tone in his voice. "That's what's keeping us from being as good as the *Lion King* performers. We're not working together."

The other kids looked at Cruz. They weren't used to him speaking up.

"He's correct," said Chloe. "So, what's going on here?" said Chloe. "Why can't you guys get it together? Cruz is learning the choreography just fine. What I'm not getting is 100 percent from the rest of you. What do we need to do to bring this show together?"

Hanna opened her mouth to speak, but Cruz interrupted her.

"Well, it's pretty obvious to me what's going on," said Cruz. "You guys don't like me. You don't want me here."

The words hung there like a rain cloud on an otherwise sunny day. Silence filled the room. No one knew what to say in response to Cruz's outburst.

Cruz got up from the floor and left the auditorium.

"Great. What do we do now?" Eva asked.

Cruz did not come back for the rest of rehearsal, so Steffan, Charisma, Hanna, and Eva worked through the show on their own. It was becoming evident that, with or without Cruz, things were falling apart fast. Even Chloe couldn't think of anything helpful to say.

"I think it's time for a team meeting," said Hanna.

At 7 P.M., she found Cruz sitting on the hotel balcony with a book.

"We need to talk to you," she said.

"What if I don't want to talk?" Cruz asked, not looking up from his book. "You have to," Hanna replied. "This group is a mess. We have to do something."

Cruz sighed and finally put down his book and came inside. The other KIDZ BOP Kids were already sitting around the living room.

"Brownie?" Eva asked, offering Cruz the plate.

Cruz took one and sat down on the couch.

"I'll start," said Hanna. "We've done some talking, and we've realized that we haven't been exactly fair to you, Cruz. We brought you here to perform with us, and things haven't exactly gone well. But we've figured out why."

"We feel guilty about replacing Elijah," Steffan blurted out suddenly. "He was an important part of our group, and when we brought you in, we all felt like we were betraying him somehow."

Eva and Charisma nodded to show that they agreed.

"This has been as hard for us as it has been for you," said Eva. "I know it hasn't seemed that way, but it's the truth."

"Sure," said Cruz, dismissively. That wasn't how it seemed to him.

"Listen," said Steffan. "I know I've been kind of a jerk to you. I just felt like a slime replacing Elijah. I didn't know what to say to him or to you. But, for what it's worth, I'm sorry, man."

"So am I," said Hanna.

"What we're trying to say," said Charisma, "is that we need you. We can't put on this show without you."

Cruz had sat silently with his arms crossed up until that point. Everyone sat, waiting for him to speak. "Okay," he said at last. "I accept your apologies. Now, we have a show to put on soon, so what do we need to do?"

Chapter 19
T Is for Teamwork!

Charisma looped her hair back in a ponytail, just like she did every time she got ready for cheerleading practice. She intended to work hard today and show Chloe that she and the other KIDZ BOP Kids could put on the show of a lifetime, and putting on her best cheerleading championship hair was a good way to start. They had a week and a half to prepare. Now was the time to put it all out there and do their best.

"You look cute with a ponytail!" said Eva, tugging at the end of it. "That's it. I'm putting mine up too."

"Hey, I'm not going to be left out of this new hairstyle trend," said Hanna, trailing behind. "Who has an extra elastic for me?"

Meanwhile, Cruz and Steffan were across the stage tying on their dance shoes. Since the team meeting the night before, the two seemed to be getting along better, laughing and chatting. They had even jammed together earlier that morning in the KIDZ BOP suite, Steffan on the guitar and Cruz on the harmonica. When Chloe walked in and saw all the girls wearing ponytails, she put down the papers she was carrying and tied her hair up in one as well.

"I have a good feeling about today," said Eva with a grin.

★

Chloe cut off the music in the middle of the second song.

"I just want to say," she said, "that you guys are *on fire* today. Keep it up!"

She started the music again.

"Okay, from the chorus! Five, six, seven, eight!" she called and they all began to move to the beat again.

There was no doubt about it. If anyone could pick up the choreography quickly and step into Elijah's shoes in a time of crisis, it was Cruz. He moved with that kind of rhythm that made dancing look easy. And now that the group was feeling better about the Elijah situation, they were finally able to watch their newest member dance without feelings of guilt.

"Awesome dance solo," said Hanna, bringing a bottle of water over to Cruz, sitting in his usual place on the edge of the stage for the break. "You've got rhythm."

"Thanks," said Cruz. "You've got some good moves yourself."

Hanna felt her cheeks getting red and tried to hide it as she sat down beside him.

"So, do you have any sisters or brothers?" she asked.

"No," said Cruz. "I'm an only child."

"You're lucky," said Hanna. "I have three. A twin brother and two younger siblings."

"Seriously?" Cruz asked, his eyes widening in surprise.

"Yeah," said Hanna. "Sharing a room with Eva and Charisma is no problem for me. I'm so used to sharing." She laughed.

"Steffan snores," Cruz whispered.

Hanna burst out laughing. "I knew it!" she said.

"Okay, enough break time," said Chloe, "we've got to rehearse. Next dance solo is you, Hanna. Are you ready?"

"Yep!" said Hanna springing to her feet.

That night, in celebration of a great rehearsal, the KIDZ BOP Kids headed out into Manhattan for a night on the town.

"You guys have not *lived* until you've had a cupcake from my very favorite cupcake shop. And then, we're heading to the Ziegfeld Theater for a movie on the big screen, the way they were meant to be seen," Eva said, a dreamy, faraway look in her eyes. The KIDZ BOP Kids knew the expression well. It was the one that Eva always had on her face when she talked about New York.

"Don't mind Eva," Charisma said to Cruz. "She suffers from 'I Love New York–itis.'"

Cruz grinned. He was excited to finally get out and see the city.

"Well, one day I'll come out to California, and you can give *me* the tour," said Eva, after overhearing Charisma's comment.

"You're on!" said Charisma, clapping her hands together with excitement. "We're going horseback riding first thing!"

"It's a deal!" said Eva.

Eva took the other KIDZ BOP Kids down to lower Manhattan to her favorite cupcake place. Sitting around a tiny table, they dug into their cupcakes.

"Whoa," said Steffan, licking the frosting on the top of his cinnamon cupcake. "This *is* the best cupcake I've ever had."

"I told you," said Eva.

"Just think," said Cruz. "Next Saturday at this time, we'll be onstage opening for Madison Day. I can't even believe it."

"Me neither," said Hanna.

"When do we actually start rehearsing at Madison Square Garden?" asked Charisma.

"Chloe said something about next week," Steffan replied. "But she has to work out a schedule with Madison's manager. She has to use the stage to rehearse too."

"I wonder if Jake will be there," said Hanna with a wink at Eva and Charisma. Madison had recently been spotted with a new A-list celebrity boyfriend.

"Ohhhhh, a big movie star watching our show!" Eva laughed. "I hope so."

"Girls are so weird," said Cruz to Steffan, rolling his eyes. They all laughed.

"Well, we'd better get going if we're going to make the movie on time!" said Eva.

Rehearsals for the rest of the week seemed to fly by. Soon, the KIDZ BOP Kids were working their way through them with ease.

"That was *Lion King* levels of awesome!"

Charisma said at the end of each song they performed, referencing the amazing show they had all seen. Comparing themselves to the *Lion King* dancers had become the running joke among the KIDZ BOP Kids. Like the Broadway performers, they were more than prepared to go onstage and dance their hearts out. If anyone messed up, Charisma would shout, "You're an understudy today! We can't let you go on performing like that!" with a big smile on her face.

The attitude in rehearsals had completely changed from the week before. Everyone was smiling and helping everyone else out. And huge levels of excitement had begun to build. During breaks from rehearsal, the name Madison Day was frequently uttered, along with "Madison Square Garden" and "Oh-Em-Gee!"

It seemed like nothing could come between the KIDZ BOP Kids and their Madison Square Garden performance now!

Chapter 20
A KIDZ BOP Surprise

The big performance was in three days. There would be two dress rehearsals, and then . . . the Madison Day concert.

"We're doing final fittings today!" said Chloe, strolling out onto the stage where the KIDZ BOP Kids were waiting to rehearse. "First, costumes. Then, we dance! Dress rehearsal in an hour!"

One by one, the KIDZ BOP Kids were taken to one of the dressing rooms to try on their costumes and have the final fittings done. The outfits the KIDZ BOP Kids would be wearing for the concert were about as awesome as they come. Everybody got to pick out their own clothing with a style that fit their personalities. Then, a tailor was brought in to make final alterations and prepare them for the show. Once the KIDZ BOP Kids were onstage, they didn't need to be tripping over too-long pant legs. And they all needed special pockets added to their clothing to hold and conceal microphone equipment. Their costumes were designed to a science to be comfortable and stylish onstage.

When all five KIDZ BOP Kids walked out on the stage decked out in their final outfits for the show, they looked around in awe of each other. Charisma wore a special costume designed to look like her Bobcats cheerleading uniform from back home. Steffan wore a T-shirt with a picture of John Lennon on it and a pair of tailored designer jeans. Eva wore black-and-white striped leggings with a bright blue dress and a fabulous hat with a large flower on it. Hanna was decked out in a tunic and jeans decorated with a pattern of rhinestones for just a bit of sparkle. And Cruz wore a pair of khakis with a button-up and a fedora that Eva stared at in envy until Cruz let her try it on. They were all dressed in very different styles. But the colors of their costumes complemented each other. And as a unit, the KIDZ BOP Kids looked very much part of the same group. They looked amazing and ready to perform.

"Well, now I'm nervous," said Eva, looking around at the other kids.

"Me too!" said Hanna. "Yesterday, I was just excited, but now I have butterflies."

"You won't be nervous when you're onstage," said Chloe, patting both of them on the back. "You won't even be able to see the crowd because of the lights. Just look out there and smile. Nobody will know you're nervous."

"Or you can picture the audience in their underwear," said Cruz.

Eva wrinkled her nose. "My grandparents will be in the audience!"

"Then be sure to remind them to put on clean ones before the show," Cruz replied, shrugging.

Eva and the other KIDZ BOP Kids burst out laughing.

With their first dress rehearsal finally out of the way, the KIDZ BOP Kids sat down in the auditorium seats while Chloe tested the sound system. They would be running through the whole show one more time, and there could be no mistakes. Then, they could take the rest of the day and do whatever they wanted.

"Cruz still needs a proper tour of the city," said Charisma. "How about a trip to Coney Island?"

"Sweet!" said Eva. It had been forever since she'd gone on the Cyclone roller coaster or looked out at the ocean from the top of the Wonder Wheel, the almost-100-year-old Ferris wheel.

The next morning the KIDZ BOP Kids would be heading to Madison Square Garden for a run-through of the concert on the big stage. It was their most important rehearsal yet. This afternoon represented the last free time they would have until Sunday, the morning after the concert. They had to make the most of it!

"Well, if we're going to Coney Island," Steffan interjected, "then we have to go to Nathan's Famous for a hot dog."

"Or seven hot dogs," said Cruz. "I'm starving. When's lunch?"

Hanna handed him a granola bar from her bag.

"Not for a while yet," she said. "It's only 10 A.M."

"Too bad," said Cruz, taking a bite of the granola bar. "Time goes so slow when you're hungry."

"Okay, KIDZ BOP Kids!" said Chloe from the stage, "Time to run through the show. Are you ready?"

The familiar first chords of "Bulletproof" began to play. At this point, the KIDZ BOP Kids didn't even need to think before beginning the choreography. It was as natural to them as breathing after this many rehearsals. Just as Chloe had promised from the very beginning!

Chloe had settled into a seat out in the auditorium to watch the kids perform, shouting out prompts when necessary. But they hardly needed any prompts at that point. Charisma came in on her vocal solo right at the beginning of the second verse. Her voice filled the auditorium. Eva broke into her dance solo immediately afterward, strutting upstage and grinning widely at the audience that wasn't yet there as she stepped to the music. One by one, the KIDZ BOP Kids came in right on cue. More and more they were looking like the happy and professional group that Chloe had envisioned from the start!

As the song continued, no one noticed the door at the back of the auditorium open and close. No one saw a person walk down the center aisle with a black duffel bag slung over his shoulder. None of the KIDZ BOP Kids noticed when that person set his duffel bag down next to the stage and stood to watch. No one noticed anything at all until the song ended and that person clapped loudly, a big smile on his face.

"Omigosh, Elijah!" said Hanna, the first to notice the sudden appearance of their friend.

The others turned to look.

"Yeah, surprise," Elijah said, giving them a little wave. "I'm back."

Chapter 21
And Then There Were Six . . .

The KIDZ BOP Kids rushed to the edge of the stage where Elijah stood, all uttering things like, "I can't believe you're here!" "What are you doing here anyway?" and "How's your ankle?"

"My ankle is fine," Elijah explained. "For all their X-rays, it was just a sprain. A really painful sprain, but a pretty minor one. The doctor gave me the go-ahead to get back to dancing. And basketball if I'm careful not to make anymore crash landings."

"But how did you get here?" Steffan asked.

"I flew. I left this morning," said Elijah. "Didn't you guys get my message?"

"No, we've been in rehearsal since 7 A.M.," said Charisma.

"I feel like I'm dreaming. Is Elijah really here? Maybe someone should pinch me," said Hanna.

"Well, I couldn't miss the show," said Elijah, rolling his eyes. "I hopped the first plane to New York. We need to rehearse!"

"Well, we're so glad you're here!" said Eva. She had genuinely missed Elijah, even his whoopee cushion and other annoying antics.

Up until that point, Cruz had stood awkwardly among his friends, not really knowing what to say in light of Elijah's sudden entrance.

"Is this the new guy?" asked Elijah catching sight of Cruz for the first time. "Hey, what's up, man?" He extended his hand to shake Cruz's.

Cruz smiled and shook Elijah's hand, but he was worried. Now that Elijah was back, this surely meant that there wasn't a place for him in the KIDZ BOP Kids anymore. What would he do now? The show was in less than a week.

"Welcome back, Elijah," said Chloe, joining the welcoming committee.

"Thanks! I missed you guys," said Elijah.

"Did you know about this, Chloe?" Eva asked.

"Elijah called me last night," Chloe said. "I didn't tell you because I wanted you to be surprised."

"Well, it worked!" said Charisma.

When Chloe went outside to make some calls, none of the KIDZ BOP Kids noticed Cruz get up and follow Chloe out of the theater. He needed to talk to her privately. He had a terrible feeling about how she might answer his question. Cruz found Chloe standing on the sidewalk in front of the theater. She smiled with surprise when she saw him.

"Hey, Cruz," she said.

"What's going to happen now?" Cruz asked. "I kinda need to know."

"I'm not sure," said Chloe.

"Is it possible for both of us to perform in the concert?" Cruz asked.

Chloe sighed. "Everything we've done is set for five performers. It wouldn't be easy to make the adjustments. We would probably end up just letting Elijah dance the lead."

"It doesn't even matter that I've been rehearsing with the KIDZ BOP Kids for the last two weeks?" Cruz asked, lines of annoyance growing on his forehead. He didn't need to hear Chloe respond to know her answer.

"Technically, Elijah was the first choice for that spot," Chloe replied. She hesitated and then continued, "I'm sorry, Cruz. I just don't know what else I can do. I wish I could—"

But Cruz didn't want to hear the rest of what Chloe had to say. Disappointment began creeping into the pit of his stomach.

"I'm outta here," he muttered.

When Chloe entered the theater again, the KIDZ BOP Kids were sitting on the edge of the stage in a row.

"Well, Elijah," said Chloe, "Are you ready to perform?"

"Hey," said Steffan, "Shouldn't we discuss what to do now that we have six members? The choreography was set for five people."

"Yeah," said Elijah. "We need to figure out what to do now that Cruz and I are both here."

The KIDZ BOP Kids looked around to see what Cruz thought of the situation. But he was gone. His dance bag was missing too. No one had even seen him leave.

"Where's Cruz?" said Eva.

"I think he's gone," said Charisma.

"He is," said Chloe.

"Now that Elijah is back, you won't need me," said Cruz in the message he left on Chloe's voicemail. "But tell the KIDZ BOP

Kids to have a great show. I'll hopefully see them when they come through Miami." His voice brimmed with disappointment. Cruz was definitely gone, and he hadn't even said goodbye before he left.

"I can't believe he just left like that," said Elijah. "We could have included him in the show. He's worked as hard for this as any of us."

"Not with two days to re-choreograph everything," said Chloe. "It's impossible at this point."

"Why not?" Elijah asked.

"Because I have enough to do without having to redo the entire show," Chloe replied.

"But—" said Elijah.

"Impossible," Chloe interrupted. "This is showbiz, guys. Sometimes it doesn't work out the way you want it to. Cruz is gone, and that's that. He left so that you could come back and join us again, Elijah. Now, we need to get back to rehearsing. And please no more arguments." She clicked away, back up to the stage. Begrudgingly the KIDZ BOP Kids took the stage with their manager. None of them felt very happy with her right then. And in Elijah's mind, a plan began to form.

Chapter 22
The KIDZ BOP Stowaway

Cruz was relaxing in a chair at the airport. His flight was leaving in forty-five minutes, and all he had to do was chill out and listen to music on his brand-new iPod. It was one of the great perks of being a temporary KIDZ BOP Kid. He had some great clothes to take home and a sweet new iPod. He'd even snuck out with the fedora that was part of his show costume. It was rightfully his, after all, and no one would miss it. (Chloe had said they got to keep their costumes.) Cruz had gone back to the hotel, packed his bag, and said goodbye to the hotel suite that had been his home for the last few weeks. He'd called Chloe one last time to ask her to book him a flight home to Miami. He'd even hailed his own cab to the airport like a real New Yorker. He was even flying home first class! He would at least be flying home in style.

Suddenly, his cell phone began to ring. Steffan's name came up on the caller ID. Cruz set his phone on vibrate and put it back in his backpack. He didn't like goodbyes, and he didn't really want to talk to Steffan right then.

Cruz had realized after Elijah arrived that bowing out and letting Elijah have his spot back was the right thing to do. Everyone was so happy to see Elijah. Cruz could have fought for it, arguing that he had worked hard and deserved to go onstage with his friends. But Elijah was the rightful member of the KIDZ BOP Kids. And Cruz had gotten a free vacation and some new friends out of it. He didn't need to go onstage and perform to make this experience complete. So, when no one was looking, Cruz grabbed his stuff and left. It was easier that way. If he stayed, he might have to watch the show from the audience, and Cruz couldn't handle doing that. Not after being a part of it for so long. It would hurt too much.

Cruz felt his cell phone buzz again. He took it out and looked at it again. Ten missed calls. Two more from Steffan, three from Charisma, one from Eva, one from Hanna, and two from a number not in his address book. He could only assume that those calls were from Elijah. Wow, those KIDZ BOP Kids sure didn't want him to leave without saying goodbye.

"Passenger Cruz Velasquez, please return to the ticketing area. Cruz Velasquez," came a voice over the loudspeaker.

Cruz panicked for a moment, quickly checking himself to make sure he had all his belongings and his boarding pass. Was something wrong with his ticket? He picked up his stuff and began to make his way back to the main terminal, feeling slightly nervous about what might be going on.

As Cruz re-entered the ticketing area and looked around, he could see the reason he had been paged over the loudspeaker. Actually there were five reasons. Steffan, Charisma, Eva, Hanna, and Elijah were standing near the escalator, all smiling nervously at him.

"You guys," Cruz said, as he walked toward them, "Now, I have to go through security again. You didn't have to go to all this effort to say goodbye."

"We're sorry," said Eva, "But we couldn't let you leave."

"You won't need to go through security again," said Steffan, his eyebrow raised.

"And this isn't goodbye. We're taking you back to the city with us."

"Look, I'm fine," said Cruz, his annoyance increasing. "Elijah's back, and you don't need me anymore. I'm over it. Now, let me get back to Miami."

Cruz had tried to keep his temper under control, but the sight of the five KIDZ BOP Kids, reunited and standing in front of him when all he wanted to do was leave, set him off.

"And what did you mean coming back for anyway?" he said to Elijah. "You knew that if you came back, I wouldn't be able to perform."

Elijah stepped forward. "Hey, man," he said, "For what it's worth, I'm sorry. I came back thinking that we would just all be a part of the show. I didn't know that it would be so hard to change things around to make room for both of us. I guess it was pretty selfish of me." Elijah looked down at the ground. He was more upset than anyone about Chloe's unwillingness to let Elijah and Cruz both perform.

"So, what do you want from me then?" Cruz asked. He could see now that Elijah felt bad, and that cooled his anger.

"So glad you asked!" said Charisma. "Because we have an idea."

"It will be tight quarters in here," said Steffan, "but I think the three of us can make it work. I have an extra sleeping bag."

Cruz looked around the room he had thought he had left forever and nodded. "Okay, that's fine." He still wasn't sure about all this. He didn't even know the plan, and yet he was going along with it. Cruz sighed and put his suitcase down by the bed.

Chloe was out when the KIDZ BOP Kids returned with Cruz, so she had no idea that he was back. And they hoped to keep it that way for as long as they could. If Chloe found out, she might put Cruz on a plane to Miami, and their plan would never work.

"So, are you guys going to keep me as a secret pet in your hotel room," Cruz asked, "or is there a plan here?"

"I'll let Elijah tell you," said Steffan.

"You're going to perform in the show," said Elijah. "Both of us are."

"You're kidding," said Cruz.

"Nope. We're going to re-choreograph the finale for six people. And we're going to do it ourselves," said Elijah.

The final song was one that Chloe had written especially for the KIDZ BOP Kids. It was called "KIDZ BOP World," and everyone had a dance and vocal solo in it. Then, they would all take their bows and run offstage to celebrate an amazing performance. But now that Cruz was part of the group, it required some serious adjustment to accommodate six dancers.

"I know it's not the whole show . . ." Elijah continued.

"But it's the best part of the show," Cruz finished for him, waving away Elijah's worries that he would still feel disappointed. "I'd be pretty proud to perform it with you guys. If you want me." He smiled.

"Good," said Elijah, slapping his new friend on the back.

Chapter 23
KIDZ BOP Goes Fashionista!

The KIDZ BOP Kids scooted all the furniture to one side of the hotel suite, leaving a large open space in the middle of the room.

"How long do we have until Chloe comes back?" Eva asked.

"Three hours," said Charisma, checking her watch.

Chloe was at Madison Square Garden overseeing final preparations for their dress rehearsal tomorrow. And that gave the KIDZ BOP Kids plenty of time to work on the choreography for their big finale. If they could just show her how easily they could make room for Cruz, she might even allow him to perform in the whole show.

"Why don't we just 'borrow' Chloe's keys again and use the theater," said Steffan slyly. "There's more room to rehearse there."

"Too risky," said Hanna, hooking Eva's iPod up to her speakers. "It was during the day last time we did that. There is a security guard on duty at night. Also, Chloe took the keys with her this time." Hanna laughed. Ever since they'd used Chloe's keys to get into the theater, she'd kept them in her pocket at all times, so that there could be no more surprise shows. "Okay," said Elijah looking around. "Let's line up and see what we need to do."

The KIDZ BOP Kids got in their usual lineup for the finale. Cruz stood awkwardly to the side to see where Elijah would stand. He felt strange taking the place where he usually stood.

Elijah looked up at him. "Let's do this," he said, tapping a pencil on Chloe's clipboard. "You stand there, Cruz, and I'll go here between Hanna and Charisma. Sound good?"

Cruz nodded and took his place.

"Let's run through it now and see what adjustments we need to make," said Elijah.

Eva started the music.

Elijah was a talented choreographer, despite the fact he had never done it before in his life. And soon, the KIDZ BOP Kids had worked their way through most of the finale.

"What do we do about the dance solo here?" Cruz asked.

"You take it," said Elijah. "I'll do the vocal solo."

"Sounds good," said Cruz. "But are you sure you don't want the dance solo?"

"I have plenty," said Elijah.

Elijah had soon worked it out so that at the end of the second-to-last song, they could easily move around, making room for Cruz. At dress rehearsal the next day, when the lights were down, Cruz would take the stage for the finale.

After that, it was up to Chloe. She would either love what they did or get upset that they went behind her back and changed the show around.

"What do we do if Chloe doesn't like it?" Eva asked.

"It's our show," said Steffan. "We're the KIDZ BOP Kids, and we should get some say in how the performance goes. I guess if Chloe refuses to let Cruz perform, we all refuse to perform."

The KIDZ BOP Kids all nodded in agreement.

"That's pretty risky," said Hanna.

"Sometimes you just gotta take risks," said Charisma.

"Now, we have another important thing to discuss," said Elijah. "What exactly am I going to wear for dress rehearsal?"

"Darn, he's right," said Steffan.

Chloe's plan was to just have Elijah wear Cruz's costume for the dress rehearsal and show, since they were both the same height and build.

"We'll have to do something then," said Hanna, creases of worry on her forehead. "They can't wear the same costume. That would get awkward."

At that point, Eva dismissed their worries with the wave of her hand. "This is New York City," she said. "If we need a costume, we'll get one."

"It's eight o'clock," said Cruz. "Where are you going to get one in twelve hours?"

"I just need to make a quick phone call." Eva got up and left the room.

An hour later, Elijah and Eva were standing in the family room of Eva's family's apartment.

Elijah looked around in awe at the high, chandeliered ceilings, pristine carpets, and the spiraled staircase leading to the second floor.

"Is that a Van Gogh?" Elijah whispered, pointing at one of the paintings hanging on the wall.

"No," Eva whispered in reply, "My dad painted it."

"Whoa," said Elijah.

His family's house was nice, but this place was insane! Eva's parents lived in an apartment palace. The look of awe hadn't left Elijah's face since Eva's family's butler had opened the door to let them in.

"Eva!" said a voice, and a tall, lovely woman entered the room.

Eva had barely seen her parents since KIDZ BOP rehearsals had begun. Her mom had been at a fashion show in Milan, and Eva had been busy rehearsing nonstop. But now, she and her mom hugged, happy to be reunited.

"So, what's the story here, kids?" said Eva's mom, looking at both of them curiously. "I heard we have a fashion emergency on our hands."

"Elijah needs a costume . . . by tomorrow," Eva replied. "Tomorrow morning actually."

Eva's mom laughed. "I think I know some people who can help us out."

Ten minutes later, three of Eva's mom's fashion design staff showed up carrying piles of clothing. They took Elijah's measurements. And an hour later, Elijah was decked out in a couture suit and matching vest that went perfectly with the other costumes in the show.

"You look . . . dreamy," said Eva, nodding with approval.

"You're a genius," said Elijah to Eva's mom, who waved away his compliments in a very Eva-like way. "Thank you so much!"

"Good luck tomorrow," said Eva's mom. "And I'll see you guys at the concert on Saturday."

As Eva and Elijah left the apartment, Elijah said quietly, "I don't know how I could ever repay your mom and her staff for putting this outfit together."

Eva shrugged. "She loves fashion emergencies. And, as for the staff, we gave them all tickets to the Madison Day show. Consider everyone repaid."

When Chloe arrived back at the KIDZ BOP suite that night, she didn't notice anything amiss. The furniture was back in place. Eva, Charisma, and Hanna were curled up on the sofa watching an episode of *Gossip Girl*.

Chapter 24
Green Light for the Green Room!

The morning before the big concert had arrived. Chloe ordered a huge breakfast for the KIDZ BOP Kids from room service. "I'm off to Madison Square Garden," she said. "The limo will be here at ten o'clock sharp to pick you up. Be downstairs with your costumes on. Our dress rehearsal starts promptly at eleven, so don't be late."

And with that, Chloe left in a flurry.

"Cruz!" Elijah called. "She's gone!"

Cruz emerged from his room, his dark hair disheveled from a night of losing sleep. Every little sound he heard he was sure was Chloe discovering that he was still in New York. He'd barely slept.

"Whew! I thought Chloe would never leave," he said. "I'm starving!"

And so the KIDZ BOP Kids dug into a breakfast of waffles and fresh fruit. "Good energy foods," Chloe had called them. They needed all the energy they could lay their hands on to get through the big dress rehearsal today.

★

At 9:45 A.M., all six KIDZ BOP Kids emerged from their rooms, decked out in their costumes, ready to go.

"I can't believe how good we all look!" said Charisma, looking around, taking it all in.

It was hard to believe that six months had gone by since she saw the notice posted on the KIDZ BOP website. "Wanna be a KIDZ BOP Kid? Show us your best performance!" it said. And now here they all were, ready to go out there onstage and be superstars. In the next hour, they would be onstage at Madison Square Garden.

When their limo arrived, the six KIDZ BOP Kids were standing outside waiting.

"I thought there were only five of you," Jack, their limo driver, said, smiling slyly at them in the rearview mirror as they all climbed into the car. He had been driving all of them around New York for three weeks and had even taken them out to the airport to get Cruz back after swearing that he wouldn't tell Chloe what was going on.

"Thank you for not saying anything. You're the best, Jack!" said Hanna.

"You know Chloe is going to be waiting for you at the performer's entrance," Jack said. "She's going to see Cruz when you guys leave the car."

"Great," said Steffan sarcastically. "What are we going to do now?"

"I've got you covered," said Jack. "I'll drop the five of you off, and Cruz and I will drive around the block a few times. Then, I'll let him out of the car and he can sneak in."

"Won't he be stopped by security?" Eva asked. She had to go through tight security even to visit her mom at her studio, and all of the security guards there knew who she was. She couldn't even imagine the level of security that would be at the entrances of Madison Square Garden. But there would probably be a lot, especially with Madison Day arriving soon.

Jack laughed. "Trust me. I know all those security guys. It won't be a problem."

The KIDZ BOP Kids were still nervous about the arrangement.

The blinking marquee at Madison Square Garden was flashing the name "Madison Day," as they drove past the front entrance. Her name was followed closely by "with opening performance by the KIDZ BOP Kids!"

"I just got chills!" said Charisma excitedly. "That's us! Can you believe it?"

No one else could say a word. There it was, Madison Square Garden. And they were on the marquee where the names of some of the world's greatest performers had been before.

Jack pulled up to the limo entrance around the corner and got out of the car to let the KIDZ BOP Kids out. All of them whispered a quiet thanks to him as they stepped from the car. Jack nodded, giving them a wink. Chloe was standing in the entryway waiting for the KIDZ BOP Kids just as expected. Cruz ducked down in the back seat of the car so that she wouldn't see him.

As Jack pulled away, they all crossed their fingers that Cruz would make it to the stage in time for the dress rehearsal finale.

The stage was set for the big show, and when the KIDZ BOP Kids laid eyes on it for the first time, their mouths all fell open in awe. There was an enormous sign with the words "KIDZ BOP Kids" written in lights hanging over the stage. It must have been fifty feet wide, with letters as tall as the KIDZ BOP Kids themselves.

"That is beyond awesome," said Elijah.

"Do you like it?" Chloe asked. "Wait until you see the lights during the show. You're going to be blown away."

Chloe looked at her watch. "Well," she said, "I guess it's time to show you to your dressing rooms."

Each KIDZ BOP Kid had a personal dressing room backstage. They even had names on the doors. Eva, Charisma, Hanna, Steffan, and Elijah all in a row in the long stretch of hallway.

"Hey," Hanna said pointing to another room across the hall. "Look at this one."

There, in a pink font, was the name "Madison Day."

"You mean we're going to be dressing room neighbors with . . . *Omigosh Madison Day???*" Charisma exclaimed in one breath.

"It's just her name," Eva reminded her, chuckling as she patted her excited friend on the shoulder. "Madison's not in there yet. She's in Boston for a concert tonight."

"You'll need to be in your dressing rooms by six tomorrow night," said Chloe. "You will all have professional stylists for your hair and makeup."

"Well, not us guys," said Elijah. "We're not wearing makeup." He paused, "Right?"

Chloe laughed. "Just stage makeup," she said. "No mascara or lipstick, I promise you."

Elijah sighed in relief.

Chloe smiled, amused by his reaction.

She didn't know that Elijah was sighing because miraculously their usually very astute manager was too busy to notice his last-minute change of costume.

Chapter 25
It's Not Over Until
Everybody Sings . . .

When the lights went up on their dress rehearsal, the five KIDZ BOP Kids were on the stage ready to perform. But every single one of them was thinking about Cruz and hoping that he would be onstage when the final song began. If he didn't make it, their plan would fall to pieces. They just had to trust that Jack would be able to get him through security.

The music began to play, and the KIDZ BOP Kids moved through the songs, one after another. No one made a mistake. This was the big time now! They were beyond mistakes at this point. And Chloe was right. With the bright stage lights in their faces, they couldn't even see out into the seats. So, fans or no fans, there were no eager faces to make them nervous. The only thing making them nervous now was the finale.

At the end of the second-to-last song, the lights went dark, and Elijah took his new position between Charisma and Hanna. Every single set of hands on the stage wore a crossed set of fingers. And right before the lights went back up again, Eva felt a tiny nudge in the darkness that told her that Cruz had arrived and was in place.

"Glad you could make it," she whispered into the darkness.

"Me too," said Cruz.

The lights came on, the music began, and the six KIDZ BOP Kids sang and danced their hearts out.

They took their bows. The crew all applauded for them; a few of them even whistled appreciatively. With the lights still in their faces, the KIDZ BOP Kids could not see Chloe, or her reaction to their surprise guest performance. But they finished their bows, waved to the empty seats as Chloe had instructed, and left the stage.

They had all agreed to meet up in Charisma's dressing room to wait for Chloe. Any time now she would be arriving, either furious with all of them for undermining her authority as their manager or slightly more willing to fit Cruz into the show because of that knock-out finale.

"Great show, you guys!" Hanna said, offering high-fives all around. "We did it."

"Way to cut it close," Steffan said to Cruz, with a grin.

Cruz laughed. "Sorry. Jack's security friend went off duty right before we got there, and the new guy did not want to let me in."

"How did you get in then?" Eva asked.

"Madison Day's manager snuck me in by telling them I was her son," Cruz explained. "Turns out, she's totally from Miami, and she's a *huge* Marlins fan. Would you believe she saw me on TV a few weeks ago? What a cool lady! Oh, and she wishes us the best of luck tomorrow night."

"What's he talking about?" Elijah asked. The other KIDZ BOP Kids just laughed.

Chloe was pretty mad.

"I can't believe you guys," she said, shaking her head. "You have undermined me time and again. I say, 'No! We can't do that' and you go right on ahead and do it anyway."

"We just wanted Cruz to be a part of the group," said Elijah. "He deserves it."

"Do you know how much time I spent choreographing all of those songs?" Chloe asked, looking around at all of their faces. For the first time since they had started rehearsing with Chloe, she looked genuinely tired. When she had walked into Charisma's dressing room, the first thing she did was flop down into a chair and sigh loudly. She didn't even speak for at least a minute. She seemed too worn out to even yell at them at this point.

"They'll have to redo the light design and everything," said Chloe. "And we'll need to run through all of this again *today*. Are you prepared to do the work necessary for this?"

"Of course we are," said Charisma. "We wouldn't have made this plan if we weren't willing to devote more time to it."

"I'll have to arrange for a dressing room for Cruz. And a . . . wait a minute. Where did you get that costume, Elijah? Is that new?"

"Eva's mom fixed me up last night when you were gone," Elijah replied. "Do you like it?"

"You guys are full of surprises," said Chloe, shaking her head. "I don't know why I'm saying this, but, Cruz, at least for tomorrow tonight, you're a KIDZ BOP Kid. Now, let's get ready for the show."

With Chloe's help, rearranging the choreography for six people was a breeze. They could all see now why she was considered one of the top choreographers on Broadway and why they were lucky to have her.

"Okay, Eva, when you do this turn, move back two steps, and we should be able to make room for Cruz," Chloe said.

They had all convened back at their rehearsal theater to go through the choreography one last time. Chloe had not even bothered to change into her dance outfit and was running through the show with them in the tailored business suit she wore for meetings. She had even taken her hair out of her usual bun and let Eva style it into braids.

"Now, we should talk about solos. Who's taking what? Elijah? Cruz? It's up to you," Chloe said.

"We worked that out already," said Elijah. "Everybody is giving up one dance solo and one vocal solo so that Cruz can have it."

"That works for me if it's okay with you guys," Chloe said, looking into their faces for approval.

"No problems here," Steffan said.

At the end of the day, all of the KIDZ BOP Kids' songs were rearranged, and they ran through the show twice on the rehearsal stage to make sure they had it down. With the combined energy of Cruz and Elijah, the performance was even better than it was before. Even Chloe noticed it.

"Well, I think we're ready for Madison Square Garden," said Charisma.

Chapter 26
The Curtain Goes Up

The day of the concert had arrived at last.

The KIDZ BOP Kids were all up and dressed in their finest pre-performance attire.

The KIDZ BOP Kids' families had all arrived in New York for the show and had all met and went out on a sightseeing tour of the city, guided by Eva's parents, before the concert that night. The KIDZ BOP Kids had barely had a chance to say hello before being pulled away for something else.

Reporters came and went, sitting the KIDZ BOP Kids down for an interview and asking them questions about the concert. "Had they met Madison Day?" "Were they excited to meet Madison Day?" "What did they think Madison Day would say about their performance?"

"Lots of questions about Madison Day," Cruz remarked, grinning.

"I'm sure all the questions she's getting are about us," said Elijah, with a nod. "'So, what do you think about working with the KIDZ BOP Kids, Tay? Is that Elijah good-looking or what?'"

"'Elijah who?'" said Charisma in her best Madison Day voice. "'Oh, that guy? He's okay. Kind of weird.'"

The other KIDZ BOP Kids laughed, including Elijah. "You haven't seen me dance yet, Madison Day," said Elijah, with a sly grin.

Their dressing rooms were all prepped for them when the KIDZ BOP Kids arrived at Madison Square Garden a few hours before the show. Their costumes were all pressed and laid out. And flowers and gifts from family members lined the room.

"Gift baskets!" Hanna exclaimed as she rushed into her dressing room. "Aw, and a 'good luck' teddy bear from my mom and dad!"

Next door, Eva dug through her gift basket to check out the goods.

"There must be six shades of lip gloss in here!" she called so that Hanna could hear her. "Who are these from?"

"They're from me," said Chloe, appearing in the doorway of Eva's dressing room. "You can't be a proper opening act without a big goodie basket."

Eva rushed to give the KIDZ BOP manager a hug. "You're the best," she said. "And not just because of the gift baskets."

"Is this brand-new whoopee cushion from you, Chloe?" Elijah asked, appearing in the doorway behind Chloe, holding up his new prize.

Chloe smiled.

"Use it wisely," she said. "And not on me."

The rest of the KIDZ BOP Kids came over to thank their manager as well. She waved off their thanks. "I wanted to do it," she said. "You've worked hard, and now it's time to enjoy it a little."

"Chloe, you're needed onstage!" said a voice, and for the first time the KIDZ BOP Kids noticed that their manager was carrying a walkie-talkie.

"I have to go check on some things. I'll be back in time for warm-ups!" And with that the KIDZ BOP Kids' manager disappeared down the hall.

Charisma was trying out the new perfume that Chloe had added to her gift basket when a small, thin, dark-haired woman arrived in her doorway.

"Charisma?" the woman asked.

"Yes," said Charisma.

"Anandi," the woman said, shaking her hand. "I'm your stylist. Are you ready to get pretty?"

Charisma nodded eagerly.

The KIDZ BOP Kids spent the next hour being prepared for the show by their individual stylists. When they each emerged from their dressing room, none of them could believe their eyes. Charisma's hair had been styled in long waves. Hanna's hair was perfectly straight and shiny. Her eyelids shone with just the tiniest amount of glitter. The stylist had done something to make Eva's already curly hair twice as curly and then fastened her hat to it so that it wouldn't come off as Eva danced. She was wearing one of the pink lip glosses from her gift bag. Charisma and Hanna pulled out the necklaces Eva had made to show Eva that they were all wearing them. Eva showed her necklace as well, and the three girls hugged.

Steffan's hair, which was usually long and rather shaggy was even trimmed and styled.

"Is that . . . product in your hair, Steffan?" Eva asked, teasing him.

"Yeah, can you believe it?" Steffan replied, touching his hair self-consciously, a shy grin on his face.

"Thirty minutes, KIDZ BOP Kids!" said a voice in the hallway. A woman wearing a headset charged by, carrying a clipboard. They smiled at her to let her know they had heard.

"Whoa," said Cruz, smoothing his own freshly styled hair and putting on his fedora. "Time sure flies when you're having fun."

"Hey, look at that," said Charisma, pointing.

The door to Madison Day's dressing room was shut tight, and a security guard was posted outside.

"She's in there!" Eva whispered loudly.

But the KIDZ BOP Kids didn't get a chance to hang out and see if they would catch a glimpse of Madison Day in person. Chloe showed up to take them to the rehearsal room to warm up and tell them their instructions for after the concert.

"Have a great show," Chloe said. "Remember what I've taught you, and you'll be fine."

The KIDZ BOP Kids nodded.

"Most importantly," Chloe added, "the limo will be waiting just outside to take you to the after-show party. I'll meet you there."

"After-show party?" Steffan asked.

"Hey, we deserve one. We're famous now," said Cruz.

The stage was set, and the KIDZ BOP Kids were on it, waiting for the lights to go up. They had gotten through some really great (and some really difficult) times together. There had been practical jokes, arguments, laughs, hugs, and even an ankle injury. And now, all six KIDZ BOP Kids stood in the darkness on the stage at Madison Square Garden. Somewhere backstage, Madison Day, one of the greatest superstars of their time, was soon going to be listening to their performance. Would she love it? Would she hate it? There was no way to know. But what the KIDZ BOP Kids did know was that they were about to give the performance of their lives.

The lights went up. The music began, and the KIDZ BOP Kids began to perform.

Chapter 27
It's a KIDZ BOP World!

The after-show party took place on the roof of a posh hotel in downtown Manhattan. The KIDZ BOP Kids settled around an elegantly decorated table and drank ginger ale brought to them on a tray by a man wearing a tuxedo.

"I'll have extra cherries in mine," said Elijah, with a grin. A moment later, the waiter returned with a bowl of cherries just for Elijah. This was the life! Ginger ale, tuxedoed waiters, and all the cherries he could ever want!

The KIDZ BOP Kids recognized some of the guests milling around as celebrities, but all of them were too shy to say hello. When Charisma came back from the bathroom, she was positively jittery when she said, "I think Lady Gaga just held the bathroom door for me!"

"She's here?" Hanna squealed.

The other KIDZ BOP Kids leaned in to listen to the full account and looked around eagerly to see if they could spot the pop icon in the crowd.

Chloe arrived to find the KIDZ BOP Kids still in a complete state of awe about their surroundings. And things were about to get even more awesome. Chloe brought with her to the table a young woman that every one of the KIDZ BOP Kids recognized immediately. She had long blond ringlets and a big smile on her face.

"KIDZ BOP Kids? This is Madison Day," Chloe said. "Madison, meet Steffan, Charisma, Cruz, Elijah, Hanna, and Eva."

"My opening act!" said Madison excitedly, shaking hands all around.

It turned out that Madison Day was loads of fun to hang out with. She posed for pictures with each of the KIDZ BOP Kids and was a good sport when Charisma nearly spilled her ginger ale on her giving her one of the famous Charisma hugs.

"I'm sorry I didn't get to meet you guys before the show," Madison said. "I had a press conference, and then I had to rehearse. But I couldn't go a minute longer without saying hello and telling you what an amazing show you put on tonight."

"You too," said Eva. She felt very shy, which was a rare occurrence for Eva.

Even Elijah, who rarely was at a loss for words, seemed awestruck into silence in the presence of the pretty songstress.

The KIDZ BOP Kids' only disappointment was when Madison announced that she had to leave the party early so that she could get ready for a concert in Philadelphia the following night. She signed an autograph for each of them, said, "See you at the Grammys!" and was gone.

"We're going to the Grammys?" Hanna asked, her eyes wide.

"If we're lucky," said Chloe.

"The reviews are in!" said Eva, holding up a copy of the *New York Times*. She'd run down to the hotel lobby first thing the next morning to buy one, still wearing her slippers.

The KIDZ BOP Kids flipped through the paper looking for the concert reviews in the Entertainment section.

Eva leaned over the paper and began to read, "The KIDZ BOP Kids, the wunderkind pop group, showed NYC last night that they know how to perform with the big dogs. When they left the stage, fans who were originally there to just see Madison Day began to chant 'KIDZ BOP Kids! KIDZ BOP Kids!' In a dynamo performance featuring six amazing dancers (I thought there were five members, but I guess I was wrong!) the KIDZ BOP Kids brought down the house. We can only hope that they will be returning to New York for a follow-up performance (this time as the headliners) very soon."

"All of the blogs are reviewing the performance too," said Charisma, leaning forward to read the screen on her laptop. "Kidnooz gave us five stars! They gave Justin Timberlake four two months ago."

"This is unbelievable," said Steffan.

Very soon after they read their reviews, the basket of gifts arrived from Madison Day.

"Tay is so sweet!" said Charisma, holding up a box of chocolates that Madison had sent over. Ever since their meeting the night before, Charisma was talking about Madison Day like an old friend. It made the other KIDZ BOP Kids smile.

The only person who seemed sad the morning after the concert was Cruz. Tomorrow, the other KIDZ BOP Kids would be heading out on their big North American tour. Cruz would be heading home to Miami. There was only room for five KIDZ BOP Kids. The New York concert had been the exception, but now that Elijah was back, a sixth group member was not needed. Chloe had been adamant, but apologetic, when she told Cruz and promised to put him in touch with her theater contacts in Miami.

Cruz was packing up one last time, feeling a bit sad about going back to Miami, but happy that he would get to see his mom again. He'd had a great time with the KIDZ BOP Kids. He'd performed onstage at Madison Square Garden! He'd met Madison Day. But now he needed to get back to Miami. He even had plans to try out for a local dance troupe. It was worth a shot, right?

When Cruz walked into the main room of the suite, pulling his suitcase behind him, he was met with the strange sight of the other five KIDZ BOP Kids sitting around the table staring at him.

"What? Do I have pillow marks on my face?" Cruz said, self-consciously.

"No!" said Hanna with a laugh. "But we do need to talk to you."

Cruz pulled up a chair at the table and sat down.

"Actually, we have a proposal for you," said Elijah. "We've talked to Chloe about it, and we would like you to join the tour. We want you to be our back-up dancer."

"Yeah, right," Cruz said. "Chloe would never go for that. She already bought me my plane ticket."

"But she did go for it," said Eva. "We told her that none of us would be performing if you couldn't come with us."

"She got pretty mad," said Elijah with a chuckle.

"That was because you put a rubber mouse in the bottom of her purse," Eva reminded him.

"Oh, yeah," said Elijah, with a little smirk.

"Nice one," Cruz said, giving him a high five.

"So, what do you think?" Hanna asked.

"I don't know what to say," said Cruz. "I am honored." He was silent for a moment. "How could I say no to you guys? You're my best friends."

"So, you'll join us?" said Steffan.

"Of course," said Cruz. "But I would like to visit my mom before I head out on tour."

Elijah laughed. "No problem, dude. Our first stop on the tour is Miami. You're golden."

"Oh! I almost forgot. Chloe said that if you're coming with us, you'll have to get a passport."

"Why's that?" Cruz asked

"Because in three months, we're heading out on our European tour," said Charisma. "And after that, who knows? Maybe Japan?"

"Apparently that's what you do after you put on the performance of a lifetime at Madison Square Garden," said Hanna. "Go out on a headlining tour."

"Well, what are we waiting for?" Cruz asked. "Let's go!"

Get an awesome
FREE KIDZ BOP song!

JUST FOLLOW THESE SIMPLE STEPS:

1. Go to *www.KIDZBOP.com/KidzBopBooks*
2. Enter your 10-digit code
3. Click "Submit"
4. Choose the KIDZ BOP song you'd like to download
5. Once your FREE KIDZ BOP download is complete, rock out!